"You've changed your mind about marrying me,"

Jake said quietly.

Josie's initial answer was a small shrug and an even smaller nod. "Uh-huh. I mean, yes. That is, you do still need a wife in order to keep your land, don't you?"

"Yes, I do."

Her hand fluttered to her throat. "Thank God." The flush climbing up Josie's neck looked red-hot. "I didn't mean that the way it sounded," she whispered.

Jake studied the woman who had just agreed to marry him. Her hair was windblown, her face clean-scrubbed and youthful. He sensed she wasn't a woman who was accustomed to asking for help. He knew the feeling. Yearning washed over him. Since he knew better than to allow himself to be distracted by romantic notions, he concentrated on the way he was responding physically, and pretended he didn't notice the inkling of hope that seemed to have found its way into his chest....

Dear Reader,

Silhouette Romance blends classic themes and the challenges of romance in today's world into a reassuring, fulfilling novel. And this month's offerings undeniably deliver on that promise!

In *Baby, You're Mine*, part of BUNDLES OF JOY, RITA Award-winning author Lindsay Longford tells of a pregnant, penniless widow who finds sanctuary with a sought-after bachelor who'd never thought himself the marrying kind...until now. Duty and passion collide in Sally Carleen's *The Prince's Heir*, when the prince dispatched to claim his nephew falls for the heir's beautiful adoptive mother. When a single mom desperate to keep her daughter weds an ornery rancher intent on saving his spread, she discovers that *McKenna's Bartered Bride* is what she wants to be...forever. Don't miss this next delightful installment of Sandra Steffen's BACHELOR GULCH series.

Donna Clayton delivers an emotional story about the bond of sisterhood...and how a career-driven woman learns a valuable lesson about love from the man who's *Her Dream Come True*. Carla Cassidy's MUSTANG, MONTANA, Intimate Moments series crosses into Romance with a classic boss/secretary story that starts with the proposition *Wife for a Week*, but ends...well, you'll have to read it to find out! And in Pamela Ingrahm's debut Romance novel, a millionaire CEO realizes that his temporary assistant—and her adorable toddler—have him yearning to leave his *Bachelor Boss* days behind.

Enjoy this month's titles—and keep coming back to Romance, a series guaranteed to touch *every* woman's heart.

Mary-Theresa Hussey

Mary-Theresa Hussey
Senior Editor

Please address questions and book requests to:
Silhouette Reader Service
U.S.: 3010 Walden Ave., P.O. Box 1325, Buffalo, NY 14269
Canadian: P.O. Box 609, Fort Erie, Ont. L2A 5X3

Sandra Steffen

McKENNA'S BARTERED BRIDE

Silhouette

ROMANCE™

Published by Silhouette Books

America's Publisher of Contemporary Romance

For my agent, Robin Rue.
I love listening to your slant on writing and on life....
This one is especially for you, Robin....
You know why.

 SILHOUETTE BOOKS

ISBN 0-373-19398-X

McKENNA'S BARTERED BRIDE

This edition published by arrangement with Harlequin Books S.A.

® and TM are trademarks of Harlequin Books S.A., used under license.
Trademarks indicated with ® are registered in the United States Patent
and Trademark Office, the Canadian Trade Marks Office and in other
countries.

Visit us at www.romance.net

Printed in U.S.A.

SANDRA STEFFEN

Her fans tell Sandra how much they enjoy her fictional characters, especially her male fictional characters. That's not so surprising, because although this award-winning, bestselling author believes every character is a challenge, she has the most fun with the men she creates. Perhaps that's because she's surrounded by so many men—her husband, their four sons, her dad, brothers, in-laws. She feels blessed to be surrounded by just as many warm, intelligent and funny women.

Growing up the fourth child of ten, Sandra developed a keen appreciation for laughter and argument. Sandra lives in Michigan with her husband, three of their sons and a blue-eyed mutt who thinks her name is No-Molly-No. Sandra's book *Child of Her Dreams* won the 1994 National Readers' Choice Award. Several of her titles have appeared on national bestseller lists.

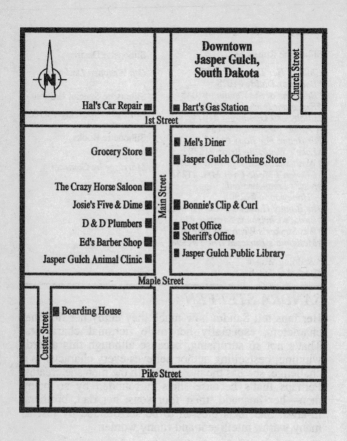

Downtown Jasper Gulch, South Dakota

Church Street

Hal's Car Repair ▪ ▪ Bart's Gas Station

1st Street

Grocery Store ▪

▪ Mel's Diner

▪ Jasper Gulch Clothing Store

Main Street

The Crazy Horse Saloon ▪

Josie's Five & Dime ▪ ▪ Bonnie's Clip & Curl

D & D Plumbers ▪ ▪ Post Office
▪ Sheriff's Office

Ed's Barber Shop ▪

Jasper Gulch Animal Clinic ▪ ▪ Jasper Gulch Public Library

Maple Street

Custer Street

▪ Boarding House

Pike Street

Chapter One

Jake McKenna felt a vibration beneath the soles of his worn cowboy boots. He lowered the tip of the pitchfork to the floor and held very still, his ears straining, his gaze trained on the patch of McKenna land visible through the wide barn door. The vibration increased. It was either a tornado, a stampede, or...

Aw, hell. He threw down the pitchfork and tore out of the barn. It was a storm, all right. A human cyclone. Sky Buchanan was racing up the lane on his horse, shoulders and head hunkered down, his hat whipping behind him, held to his body only by the cord around his neck.

Swearing under his breath, Jake rushed to the gate and swung it open five seconds before Sky rode through at breakneck speed. "Dammit all, Buchanan!" he growled as Sky pulled to a stop a few feet short of the broad side of the barn. "One of these days I'm not going to get here fast enough and I'll end up scraping you off that wood with a chisel."

Skyler Buchanan dismounted neatly, then turned on his

heels in one fluid movement. Jake narrowed his eyes and sneered. "You ever decide to turn in your cowboy boots for ballet slippers, you got the turns down pat."

Sky's smile grated on Jake's already frayed nerves. Leading his horse by the reins, Sky said, "You're trying to pick a fight. That means it's either a day that ends in y, or the reading of your old man's will didn't go so well."

Inside the barn Jake swiped his black Stetson off his head and kept the string of four-letter words running through his head to himself. Cramming his hat back on again, he retrieved the pitchfork and picked up where he'd left off.

"Jake?"

Jake's reply had a lot in common with a snort.

"What did the will say?"

The barn was quiet except for the creak of leather, the scuffle of hooves and the scrape and rustle of straw.

"Well?" Sky prodded. "Did Isaac leave the ranch to you or didn't he?"

Jake scooped up another forkful of straw and sent it sailing into one of the stalls. "More or less."

A horse whinnied; a saddle creaked. Jake knew Sky was watching him, just as he knew his best friend wouldn't ask any more questions until Jake was ready to answer. Where Sky had patience, Jake had purpose. Both would trust the other with his life.

When he'd worked the edge off his temper, Jake stuck the pitchfork into the pile of straw and looped his hands over the top of the handle. "It's pretty much black-and-white."

"Then why do you look as if you're seeing red?"

Jake shrugged, scowled. "Got me. With the exception of the hundred acres that spans Sugar Creek, my father left everything to me."

"What the hell do you—"

Finally Jake turned to face his friend. "The hundred acres that spans Sugar Creek *will* be mine. Providing I'm a married man by my next birthday."

"And if you're not a married man come July?"

Jake's eyes darkened. "Then the most fertile soil on Mc-Kenna land will go to the O'Gradys."

Sky rarely used four-letter words. He claimed he rarely needed to. He uttered one now. Jake thought it pretty much said it all. "Should have known the old cowpoke would find a way to run your life from the grave," Sky insisted.

Jake squeezed his fingers so hard into fists his square fingernails dug into the calluses on his palms. The O'Gradys owned the biggest spread in a two-hundred-mile radius and never missed an opportunity to remind the McKennas that theirs was second. Jake hated being second. In anything. But he hated being second to the O'Gradys most of all.

Jake looked over his shoulder. "Did you hear something?" he asked.

Sky made a show of listening intently. The ranch hands had all gone into Pierre to raise a little Friday night hell. A horse nickered, and the wind was picking up. The wind was always picking up in South Dakota. With a shake of his head, he primed the hand pump and said, "Are you trying to change the subject?"

Jake grunted.

"Relax. You've got some time here. It's only the first of May. You take everything so seriously."

"This is serious, dammit. Maybe you could try it yourself for ten seconds."

"I'm plenty serious. About my horse. About that calf I just helped into the world. And I'm seriously glad Isaac McKenna wasn't my father."

With the grace Skyler Buchanan had been born with and

had learned to use to his best advantage years ago, he turned on his heel and headed for the door. Watching him saunter away, Jake called, "Where are you going?"

"Thought I'd mosey on up to the house and bring back some of your old man's favorite rum. While we polish off the bottle, we can come up with a plan."

"Getting blind drunk isn't going to make me a happily married man."

"You didn't say the will stipulated that you had to be happy. I'll be right back with that bottle. I'd say you've earned it, wouldn't you?"

Jake strode as far as the door. He could see the big house from here. Isaac McKenna had purchased it and the surrounding land right after he'd gotten married almost forty years ago. He'd added a wing and the porch ten years later, just before Jake's mother had decided to run away with a man she liked better. Isaac had bought more land, but the house had remained the same as it had been for thirty years. There were no welcome mats by the doors, no flowers by the steps, no flowering bushes, nothing that added warmth or that said home.

It was Jake's now, the house, the land, the animals. He would have to do something about the stipulation in his father's will, but not tonight. Tonight, he and Sky would tie one on and try to forget about the rest.

He walked around to one side of the barn. Hitching a boot on the lowest rung of the fence, he stared at the land he'd inherited. On the horizon a herd of some of the best cattle in the West moved toward the watering hole just over the hill where they would settle down for the night. The cows whose calves were old enough to wander lowed, their offspring bawling frantically until they were reunited with their mothers. In late summer when the clouds forgot how to rain, the herds would settle on the hundred acres that spanned Sugar Creek. The hundred acres that would belong to the O'Gradys unless Jake found a wife by July.

He hoped Sky got back with that bottle soon.

Swiping his hat off his head, he let the wind blow through his hair. There were always fences to mend, machinery to fix, crops to tend. Branding was just around the corner. Except for fall, winter and summer, spring was the busiest time of the year out here. How in the hell was he supposed to free up enough time to find a wife?

Even if he had the time, Jasper Gulch had no single women. Or almost none. It wasn't a new problem for the area. Women had started leaving Jasper Gulch fifty years ago. They'd been leaving in droves the past twenty. No one could blame them. Ranch life just couldn't compete with the lure of the city and better job prospects. A few years back the town council had taken it upon themselves to advertise for women. Small newspapers had run the story. Larger papers had picked it up. Before long, Jasper Gulch had been dubbed Bachelor Gulch, and busloads of women had flocked here to check out the shy but willing men of Jasper Gulch. Most of those women had taken one look at the meager stores, the dusty roads and the even dustier ranchers and cowboys and had kept right on going. A few had stayed. Most of those had bit the dust in another way and were now married to a few of those former so-called eligible bachelors, the Jasper Gents.

Who was left?

Gravel crunched beneath Sky's boots. Choosing a section of fence a foot from Jake's elbow, Sky uncapped the rum and handed Jake a glass. "To Captain Morgan."

Glasses clinked. Both men downed the first shot.

Sky poured again. "To Isaac McKenna."

This time Jake didn't clink his glass against Sky's. He didn't waste his breath damning his father to hell, either.

Surely Isaac McKenna had found his way there all by himself.

Taking the time to appreciate the slow burn that made its way to the bottom of his stomach, Jake held out his empty glass. Sky obliged him by filling it to the rim.

"I've been thinking," Sky said.

"I'll alert the press."

"Be my guest." Sky's grin was downright wicked. "I always like a little publicity."

"What have you been thinking, Buchanan?"

"This situation of yours isn't as hopeless as you thought."

"How do you figure?"

Jake was aware of the up-and-down look Sky cast him. "I don't see it, myself," the lanky cowhand with the shock of black hair and piercing green eyes said, "but women have been known to find you attractive. I've heard more than one woman say you wear your hair a little too long to be civilized. And they weren't complaining. 'Course, there are those who think you're coldhearted like your old man. I know better, but it would help if you smiled once in a while."

"I smile."

Sky stared straight ahead. "Sure you do."

"I smile, dammit."

"When?" Sky said quietly. "When was the last time you smiled and meant it?"

Jake stared at the liquid in his glass. "It's been a while since I've had something to smile about, that's all."

Sky cocked one eyebrow just enough to make his point, and Jake said, "I think you're wrong, Sky. I think the situation really is hopeless. And so am I."

"Naw. There are still a handful of single women in Jasper Gulch."

"A small handful."

"There's Crystal Galloway."

"Crystal Galloway has as much use for men as she does for another degree."

"That's true," Sky said thoughtfully. "I can't figure that out, either. She's a looker, that's for sure. But why did she come to a town that advertised for women if she had no intention of looking for a man?"

"Who knows," Jake answered. "You were saying?"

"Oh, yeah. There's Tracy Gentry."

"She's barely out of diapers."

"She's twenty-one. For a desperate man, you're mighty choosy, McKenna. I probably shouldn't even mention Brandy Schafer, since lately she seems to have hooked up with Jason Tucker. There's that gorgeous, far-removed relative of Wes Stryker's, Meridith Warner, but to tell you the truth, I've been keeping my eye on her myself."

Jake turned his head slowly. Or at least it felt that way to him. Ah, yes, the rum was doing its job. "You finished?"

"Not quite. I suppose I could be noble and give you first dibs on Meridith."

Oh, no. Jake didn't live by many rules, but an honorable man didn't move in on another man's territory. Besides, Jake happened to know that Meridith had been keeping an eye on Sky, too. "You want her," Jake said slowly, "you go for her."

Sky looked relieved. "There is one other single woman."

"Who?" Jake downed another good portion of the spiced rum in his glass.

"Josie Callahan."

"Jo—" Jake sputtered, choked and sputtered some more.

"Well looky there. You're already out of breath just hearing her name."

Jake wheezed. He coughed. "Josephine Callahan? That's the best you can do?"

"What's wrong with Josie Callahan?"

"She's as shy as a church mouse and about as appealing. Besides, she's been in Jasper Gulch for more than a year. If she wanted to be married, she would be by now."

"Do you have a better idea?"

Jake thought about the pale little redhead who would sooner study her shoe than look at him. "Yeah," he said, shoving his glass toward Sky. "As a matter of fact I do. Fill 'er up."

Josie Callahan, indeed.

"Please let there be a mistake. Please." Josie Callahan added the column of numbers in her ledger a second time. A third time. Figuring had always been her strong suit, and today was no exception. There was no mistake. Her income didn't add up to her expenses. It was as plain as the freckles on her nose.

Shoot, shoot, shoot, shoot.

She squeezed the pencil and tried not to panic. There wasn't going to be enough money to buy much food this month, let alone enough money to pay her rent and the rest of her bills. Josie could have gone hungry, but her little girl needed to eat. Kelsey also needed a roof over her head and security, something Josie had strived to give her daughter since she'd laid big, robust Tom Callahan to rest two years ago.

Think, Josie, think.

She was good at adding and subtracting. Planning was something else again. Tom used to tell her she planned with her heart, not her mind. That's what had landed her at the altar when she was barely nineteen. It had brought her to this quaint little town in South Dakota a year ago, too.

She wasn't sorry about either of those things. No sir, she wasn't. Marrying Tom had been the best thing she'd ever done, unless she counted having Kelsey nine months to the day later. And moving to Jasper Gulch hadn't been a mistake. It couldn't have been.

"Isn't that right, Tom?" she whispered.

That's right, Josie.

She smiled the whole time she was wrapping up the loaves of homemade bread she'd baked earlier. She just couldn't help it. Unlike other widows who grew sad because they couldn't remember the sound of their husbands' voices, Josie knew exactly how Tom's voice sounded. She heard it all the time. Sometimes he only mumbled a word or two, but just the other day he'd gone on and on about how it was time for her to find another husband. He'd even told her he was going to help. She'd rolled her eyes toward the ceiling and told him she would prefer it if he would help her choose the winning lottery numbers. His laughter had carried to her ears all the way from heaven.

She was still smiling when she set the cellophane-wrapped loaves of bread in the window. Oh, she wasn't sure it was possible for a man to help a woman find a new husband, especially from the other side. She didn't want another husband, anyway. But darned if she hadn't been watching the door to her little shop on Main Street more than usual these past two days.

Several people had stopped in. Unfortunately it seemed that most of the fine folks in Jasper Gulch only wandered into the combination dime store, bakery and flower shop to hear the floor creak. If only she could come up with a way to charge for that, she wouldn't be in so much trouble right now. She'd waited on the fine folks, listened to the town gossip and tried not to worry about the future. She had to admit she'd rather enjoyed trying to figure out who Tom might pick out for her. Some of the people she'd waited on *had* been men. A few were even single men. But so far, not one of them was anybody she would want to marry— not that she wanted to marry anybody ever again.

The bell over the door jingled, and a broad-shouldered, muscularly built man paused just inside the door. Josie swallowed and quickly averted her gaze. She especially wouldn't want to marry him.

Jake McKenna. His name was as hard as the rest of him; his eyes were dark brown, his hair darker still. Although he wore it a little longer than the other men in the area, it did nothing to soften his angular face. It did nothing to alleviate the nerves that crawled up her spine every time she came face-to-face with him, either.

"Afternoon," he said, tugging once on the brim of his black Stetson.

"Hello. Can I—" She cleared her throat quietly. "That is, can I help you?" she asked, sliding her accounting underneath the counter.

"As a matter of fact, I'm hoping you can."

She didn't know what made her more nervous: his answer or the fact that he was staring at her in a very deliberate, very assessing sort of way.

"What would you like?" she asked, striving for a cheery tone. "Something baked? A bouquet of flowers? Or something from the five-and-dime end of the store?"

What did he want? Jake thought, glancing around. Now there was a question. Stalling, he peered at the glass-fronted cooler where a few scraggly bouquets of flowers sat in glass pitchers. Next he cast a glance at the bread in the window, and finally at a bin at the end of the counter containing kites and rubber balls.

"Mr. McKenna?"

He eased closer and was about to try on the smile he'd been practicing when a young voice called, "I'm all done with my painting, Mama, what can I…"

A little scrap of a girl slipped around a curtain separating the back room from the rest of the store, her question trailing away the instant she noticed Jake. "Hello," she said, smiling sweetly.

The girl looked about five or six. She wasn't pretty, exactly, but she was female all the way down to the holes in her shabby tennis shoes.

"Mama," she said without taking her eyes off Jake. "I have a joke."

"I have a customer, sweet pea."

The little girl all but batted her eyelashes. Jake knew women who could have taken lessons. One of them was in this very room.

"Wanna hear my joke, mister?"

Jake shrugged, and the little femme fatale sashayed closer. "What's Irish and stays out all summer?"

"Kelsey, honey," Josie admonished gently. "I don't think Mr. McKenna has time for jokes."

"Do you have time?" Kelsey asked.

"How long is your joke?" he asked.

"Not long."

"Okay. What's Irish and stays out all summer?"

"Patti O'Furniture."

Kelsey raised her eyebrows in silent expectation. Jake felt a strange compulsion to laugh. He would have, too, if a deep, sultry chuckle hadn't drawn his attention. Josie was bent at the waist, her face angled down toward her daughter, a shock of unruly red hair skimming her cheek. He'd thought she was shy and plain. Her laughter was neither of those things. It was uninhibited, and it filled the quiet store like a song, undiluted, marvelous, catching. A woman who could laugh like that could probably curl a man's toes in bed.

He felt a tightening in his throat and a chugging in his chest. Neither were particularly pleasurable sensations, but the strumming, thickening surge taking place slightly lower felt pretty damn good, so good in fact that he took a second look at Josephine Callahan. He still thought she was on the plain side, but now he wondered if it was the result of a lack of adornment. She wore no makeup, no jewelry, nothing that might call attention to the features of the woman inside the loose-fitting, faded dress. Her eyes were green and pretty enough, he decided, her hair a shade of red he'd never seen before. It was unusual, yes, but he'd be willing to stake his ranch that it was natural.

The ranch. That was why he was here. That, and the harebrained idea Sky had come up with to keep all of it in one piece. Suddenly it didn't seem like such a harebrained idea after all.

Josie wasn't sure why she was laughing. The joke had been silly, and yet it had struck her funny bone. Kelsey thought so, too, and was giggling for all she was worth. Her brown eyes were crinkled, her shoulders hunched forward, her head tipped back. Why, it was as if she believed the change in the atmosphere was all her doing.

The change in atmosphere? Josie straightened. The atmosphere in the tiny store *had* changed. She raised her eyes to Jake's and caught him looking. She averted her gaze hurriedly, but it seemed her traitorous eyes had minds of their own. She found herself staring up at him. She swallowed and had to force herself not to take a backward step. He was looking at her as only a man could look at a woman. And she was responding to that look.

She wasn't well.

In an attempt to tear her gaze away, she gestured to the baked goods on display beneath the glass-topped counter. "Can I interest you in a homemade pie, Mr. McKenna?"

He shifted closer. "Actually, I came in to talk to you about something." His gaze settled to her mouth, to her neck, to her shoulders. "Something important."

Josie's breath hitched. She definitely wasn't well.

"Well," she said, clearing her throat of the bothersome little frog that seemed to have gotten stuck there. "I mean, what did you want to talk about?"

"It's a private matter."

She gestured to her empty store. "It doesn't get much more private than this, Mr. McKenna."

His gaze swung to Kelsey, and Josie understood. Trying on a smile that felt a little stiff, she said, "I'm afraid I don't get complete privacy until after Kelsey goes to bed at eight."

He gave her that assessing, calculated look again. And then he said, "I'll come back later. After she's in bed. You live in the apartment above the store, right?"

"Er, I mean, yes. Yes, I do, but I don't think—" For heaven's sake, she was staring into his eyes again, wondering if he ever smiled. Her cheeks grew warm. If she wasn't careful, a blush was going to rise to her face. It might help if he would look someplace else.

As if in answer to her prayers, he reached into his back pocket and drew out his wallet. "I'll take all four loaves."

"Pardon me?"

"That homemade bread. It is for sale, isn't it?"

Josie came to her senses with a start. "Yes. Yes, of course." She scurried around the counter and took the bread from the window display. Pleased to have something constructive to do, she placed the loaves in a bag and pressed the appropriate keys on her old cash register.

"That'll be…"

He handed her a twenty before she could name the total. With a tug on the brim of his hat, he headed for the door.

"Don't forget your change, Mr. McKenna."

He turned around slowly, moving with an easy grace, a kind of loose-jointedness one automatically associated with a cowboy of old. Her breath hitched all over again.

"Keep it."

He stood half in, half out of the store, his gaze holding hers. Josie had a feeling that somewhere in the dark recesses of his mind, he knew exactly what he was doing. It was disconcerting, because she didn't have a clue.

His Stetson was well-worn and faded, and his boots looked as if they'd walked a thousand miles. Whether the man preferred to wear broken-in boots or not, they'd been expensive, and so was his hat. The McKennas could afford nice things. She couldn't even afford to buy Kelsey a new pair of shoes. That didn't mean she would accept charity.

"I can't do that. It just wouldn't be right." Luckily she was good at math and was able to draw the correct change from the drawer. She hurried around the counter and handed him his money with nimble fingers, more careful than usual, to keep contact at a minimum. "Enjoy your bread. Good day, Mr. McKenna."

"Bye, mister," Kelsey called.

He glanced at the little girl as if he'd forgotten she was in the room. And then he did what Josie had wanted him to do. He smiled. It did crazy things to her heart rate, not to mention her breathing, but it did nothing to relieve the tension filling the store.

"I'll see you later," he said. "And call me Jake."

Josie's heart thudded once, twice, three times. As one second followed another, it seemed to stop beating altogether.

She didn't know how long she stared at the door after he'd gone. She might have studied it forever if Kelsey hadn't said, "Do you think that's the man Daddy's sending to be my new father?"

Josie swung around. Goodness gracious. She placed her hands on her cheeks and told herself to stop being silly. Wondering if it might have been wiser if she'd kept that particular tidbit of information from Kelsey until Josie had had more time to think about it, she glanced over her shoulder where she could see Jake McKenna pulling out of his parking space in front of her store.

His truck was black and shiny and expensive looking. She thought it suited him. He rested one arm along his open window and steered with the other hand, maneuvering out of the tight spot with ease. Josie turned her back on the view. He might have had the looks, the style, and oh, yes, the moves to unsettle a feminine heart, but that didn't mean he had unsettled hers.

"Do you, Mama?" Kelsey prodded.

"I'm afraid not, sweet pea. Surely the man Daddy would like us to find will be more like Daddy."

Kelsey stared into Josie's eyes for a long time. Sighing, she lowered her chin forlornly and murmured, "I hope Daddy hurries."

The nerves that had been clamoring the past few hours stilled. Tenderness filled her heart and thickened her throat. She and Kelsey might have been down on their luck. They might have even been a little desperate. But she thanked her lucky stars for her blessings, especially for this sweet, inquisitive, adorable child.

Josie reached beneath the counter for her ledger and quickly jotted down the amount of money she'd just received from Mr.—er, Jake McKenna. Maybe she couldn't give her child another father, and Lord only knew what she was going to do about her bills, but she would use the money she'd just received to pick up a few groceries and prepare her daughter a nutritious meal.

That sense of calm had started to wane by seven-thirty. Now, an hour later, it was completely gone. Josie took a deep breath, trying to blame the queasy sensation in her stomach on the peanut butter sandwich she'd eaten when Kelsey hadn't been looking. Josie strode to the refrigerator and peered inside. Even the sight of the half gallon of milk and the leftover spaghetti and meatballs Kelsey would eat tomorrow didn't chase her unease away. This unease had nothing to do with money. It had to do with…

Josie gulped.

It had to do with the knowledge that Jake McKenna was due to arrive any minute. At the sound of footsteps on the stairs, her nerves clamored even more. Make that any second.

She knew the knock on her door was forthcoming. She still jumped when it sounded. She didn't understand it. She was never this high-strung. Lifting her eyes to the ceiling, she whispered, "If this is your idea of a joke, Thomas Callahan, it isn't funny."

Waiting until the old clock that had belonged to her parents had finished chiming the half hour, she took a deep breath for courage and opened the door just in time to see Rory O'Grady stepping off the bottom step and Jake McKenna standing on the top one.

"Mr. McKen—"

"What the hell was *he* doing here?"

The anger glittering in Jake's eyes sent her heart to her throat and her stomach into a tailspin. This time there was no stopping her backward step.

Pushing the door all the way open, he marched inside, turning the inch her tiny retreat had given him into a mile.

Chapter Two

Jake stormed past Josie so quickly the hem of her dress ruffled in his wake.

"Won't you come in, Mr. McKenna?"

He got as far as the middle of her living room before he swung around and glared at her. At least her sarcasm hadn't been wasted on him. She reached for the doorknob to close the door, glancing down the stairs at the last minute. Rory was looking up at her, a big old smile on his friendly face. Josie couldn't help smiling right back. That smile slipped a full two notches when she turned her attention back to the angry man in her living room.

She didn't have a lot of experience dealing with angry men. Her father had died when she was small, and Tom had had an easygoing, pleasant disposition. She folded her arms and stood as tall as her five-foot, three-inch frame would allow. "Would you like to sit down, Mr. McKenna?"

"I asked you to call me Jake."

Josie met his stare head-on. "You *told* me to call you Jake."

His eyebrows rose slightly, then lowered, a muscle working in his jaw. There was inherent determination in the set of his chin, and more than a hint of impatience everywhere else. As one second followed another, his expression changed in the subtlest of ways. He didn't smile, exactly, but he unclenched his teeth and removed his hat.

"A friend of mine keeps telling me that my people skills need a little work."

Josie tried to square her shoulders against his allure. It worked, for about five seconds, and then she had the most amazing urge to grin. She didn't, of course. She'd read somewhere that loss and pain and suffering built character. At least it had been good for something.

"Would you mind telling me what Rory O'Grady was doing here, Josephine?"

His use of her given name was nearly her undoing. "I might, if you can show me what it has to do with you."

Jake considered several replies, discarding them one after the other. For the first time since setting foot inside the apartment, he took note of his surroundings. Green curtains, the kind that never wore out, hung at the windows. The couch was threadbare, the pictures on the wall were cheap prints. Even the afghan folded over the back of the couch looked as if it had seen better days. The same could have been said for Josie's dress. Shy, plain Josie Callahan. That was how people described her. She was quiet, he decided, not shy. And it was amazing how that little flare of temper transformed her common face into something so uncommon.

He placed his hat on the table and settled his hands on his hips. If his plan had a snowball's chance in hell, he was going to have to make amends. It was something the

McKennas had never been very good at. "Maybe it isn't any of my business, but Rory O'Grady is a noted womanizer, and you wouldn't be the first woman he took for a ride."

"I'm a grown-up," she said, head held high. "Besides, something tells me I'm the first woman he's asked to marry him."

Jake blinked as if she'd flung ice water in his face. Outwardly he remained calm. Inside, his stomach roiled. Suddenly the noise he'd thought he'd heard Friday night and the fact that the drifter he'd hired last week hadn't shown up for work on Saturday and was now working for O'Grady made sense. The cowhand must have been eavesdropping and had run straight to O'Grady with his information. Damn. Jake had intended to ease into this, maybe take Josie out a few times, get to know her and vice versa before springing his marriage proposal on her. Leave it to that stinking O'Grady to beat him to it.

He hadn't been aware that he'd paced to the window until he caught sight of his reflection in the glass. "Did you say yes?"

"I don't even know him."

He drew in a deep breath and forbade himself to appear too relieved. There wasn't much he could do about the smug feeling of satisfaction settling in where his agitation had been. He turned slowly and said, "Of course you don't."

Josie regarded Jake quizzically for a moment. His voice had been calm, his gaze steady, but his smile made her suspicious. He wasn't a man prone to smiling. In a strange way, she felt honored to be on the receiving end of such a rare occurrence. It forced her to take a closer look at him. On the outside he was all planes and angles and five-o'clock shadow, but there was more to him than appearances. Underneath, he was a man. Not just any man, but a lonely one.

That got to her, because Josie Callahan was on a first-name basis with loneliness. However, it wasn't loneliness that had her eyelids lowering, her breath catching in the back of her throat, and something she barely recognized shifting low in her belly. She bit her lip and tried to avert her gaze. Strangely, she couldn't move.

"Would you have dinner with me tomorrow, Josephine?"

Nobody, but nobody, called her Josephine. She'd always hated her full name. And yet when he said it, it sounded sensual, feminine, alluring. "Dinner?" she heard herself asking.

"Yes. You do like to eat, don't you?"

Her gaze caught on his mouth, and she found it wasn't easy to speak. "I've already made plans to have dinner with Rory tomorrow night."

The room, all at once, was very quiet.

Jake took a very large, very deliberate step toward her. "I thought you said you didn't agree to marry him."

"I said I don't even know him. I didn't say I wouldn't have dinner with him."

Jake's face hardened, and suddenly Josie was glad she'd made other plans. Oh, she had a feeling he was right about Rory O'Grady. The man was smooth and attractive and just cocky enough to be a bit of a rogue. She wasn't worried about handling him. Handling Jake McKenna would have been another story.

"You're seeing O'Grady now, is that it?"

"Does that bother you?"

Bother him? He'd passed *bothered* the instant he'd met O'Grady on the stairs. Hell, Jake was well on his way to full-scale frustration.

"Now why on earth would that bother me?" He reached the table in three strides, cramming his hat on his head while he headed for the door. "Like you said, you're a grown woman."

And O'Grady was a grown man. Jake swore under his breath. At this rate, Rory was going to end up with Jake's hundred acres and one of the few single women left in Jasper Gulch. Anger crashed through Jake, straight as a shot of whisky right out of the bottle. He supposed he could put up a fight, but he'd be damned if he would be second.

Josie watched him go, flinching when the door closed just short of a slam. Whew. She was lucky to have escaped without having her ears singed. She locked the door, then stood leaning against it, thinking. Jake McKenna was a very formidable, intimidating man. His face was too hard, and he smiled too little.

And he'd left without saying goodbye.

The crowd at the Crazy Horse Saloon was typical for a Tuesday night. It consisted of a dozen men who moved slow, drank slow, and were slowly driving Jake nuts. Their outlook was gloomy, their small talk annoying. Which was why he normally preferred to drink alone. He might have done that, too, if Sky hadn't given him a lecture about the dangers of that kind of drinking and that kind of thinking.

Sky Buchanan would make a good old woman. Unfortunately, or was it fortunately, Jake wondered, staring into his untouched beer, Sky was also the best cowhand he'd ever had, not to mention the closest thing to a brother Jake had had in a long, long time.

Jake had listened to Sky. As a result he'd wound up at a table for one in the Crazy Horse Saloon, nursing a beer and trying not to pay attention to the only topic of conversation the local boys seemed interested in. Josie Callahan and Rory O'Grady.

"I hear tell Rory sweet-talked her into having dinner with him in Pierre."

"I know. And she agreed. Shoot. I shouldn't have waited so long."

"That Rory sure has a way with women."

"That's true, but I can't quite picture him and Josie, eh, you know what I mean."

Jake tipped his head back and let the beer drizzle down his throat, trying not to listen.

"You holler when you're ready for another, okay sugar?" DoraLee Brown asked the instant he lowered the half-empty bottle to the table. He nodded, and she winked. Jake felt a little better. Leave it to DoraLee to know what he needed.

He'd always liked DoraLee. All the men in Jasper Gulch did. Most of them had had a crush on her at one time or another. Forget the fact that she was twenty years older than half the men in the room. There was just something about a voluptuous, bleached blonde serving up beer and whisky with a smile that instilled romance in the hearts of men of all ages. A couple of years back, one of those men, Boomer Brown, had finally talked her into romancing him. Boomer and DoraLee had eloped soon after, which was good for Boomer, and DoraLee had never looked happier. Now there was one less single woman in town.

"I don't know," Forest Wilkie complained from a table up front. "Josie doesn't seem like Rory's type to me."

Great. They hadn't gone on to another topic.

"*Every* female is Rory's type."

DoraLee clucked her tongue. "Can't you boys think about anything else?"

Yes, Jake thought, reaching for the ice-cold bottle of beer in front of him. That DoraLee was all right.

"What else is there?" Neil Anderson grumbled.

A few other men mumbled in agreement, and Forest continued in the same vein. "It's just that Rory and Josie are complete opposites. I mean, nobody was surprised when our very own Melody McCully married Clayt Carson. 'Cepting maybe Clayt. And do you know why? Because they're two peas in a pod."

"Sometimes opposites attract," Cletus McCully, Melody's grandfather said, his thumbs hooked around his navy blue suspenders.

"That's true," Forest agreed. "Look at Lisa and Wyatt. He's one of the leaders of our fine community, and he up and married a girl who had a reputation."

"A reputation Lisa didn't earn," DoraLee admonished.

"Yes," Forest said, "but Rory's earned his. That man's a hound dog if there ever was one."

"Anybody hear a weather report lately?" Jake asked.

Forest looked at him in an abstract, absent sort of way. "There's a chance of rain all week. The point I'm tryin' to make is this."

Jake scowled into his beer. Nobody took longer to make a point than Forest Wilkie.

"I can't see Rory settling down with sweet, shy Josie Callahan. He's sown some pretty wild oats, and—"

"He's probably sowing a few more tonight," Neil cut in.

Jake rose to his feet so fast his chair shot out behind him. He was aware of the gazes following him as he dropped a few bills on the counter and headed for the door. He'd reached the sidewalk out front when one of the other Anderson brothers' voices carried through the open door.

"Guess we scraped a raw nerve."

"It ain't hard to do. Jake's got more raw nerves than an open wound."

Jake scowled as he opened the door on his truck. Hiking one boot on the dusty running board, he happened to glance up at the window over the dime store next door. The upstairs apartment was dark. Must be Rory and Josie weren't back yet. Unless they were back and hadn't bothered turning on the lights.

He hauled himself into his seat, slammed the door and started the engine. The patch of rubber he laid squealing away from the curb didn't curtail his frustration in the least. He rounded the corner, opened his window and cranked up the volume on the radio. The village limit sign was up ahead. Beyond it stretched miles and miles of empty highway. He pressed his foot to the accelerator and headed for the open road where he could drive until he'd taken the edge off his agitation. He figured a hundred miles might do it.

The wind was warm, the music was loud, his truck was running like a well-tuned machine. Ah. This was more like it. Those rough edges were already starting to dissolve.

His mind wandered to the ranch, the herd, his horse, the conversation he'd overheard in the Crazy Horse. *That man's a hound dog if there ever was one.* Jake imagined O'Grady putting the moves on Josie. Rory had always been a smooth talker. He'd been known to brag that he could get a woman out of her clothes in fifteen seconds or less. Jake imagined Rory trying to get Josie out of hers. He slammed on the brakes and made a U-turn before he could wipe the image from his brain.

He killed the radio and drove back into town in silence, his agitation more prickly than ever. The first thing he noticed when he pulled into the alley that ran behind the buildings on the east side of Main Street was the shiny red truck parked near Josie's back stairs. The second thing he noticed was the light in the window overlooking the alley. Had they just gotten back? Or had they just turned on the light?

Jake pulled into the shadows behind the Crazy Horse Saloon. Strumming his fingers on the steering wheel, he told himself he was only there to make sure O'Grady brought Josie home safe and sound.

He turned off the engine and heaved a deep sigh. He was no better at lying to himself than he was at lying to anybody else.

He and Rory had always been rivals. Jake didn't know how it had started, but he distinctly remembered the day it had come to a head. He and Rory had both been twelve. They'd buried Jake's brother a few weeks earlier, and Jake was feeling surly. Mrs. Fergusson had just announced that parents' night was coming up. Rory had leaned over and whispered, "Guess your mother won't wanna leave her rich boyfriend down in Texas to come. My father says a woman who takes money for sex is a whore whether she's on a street corner or in a penthouse."

Jake had gotten a week's detention for breaking Rory's nose. Neither of them had ever apologized, and they'd never been friends since.

Rory O'Grady had always been cocky and arrogant and conceited. But he wasn't an ax murderer or a rapist. The O'Gradys were braggarts, not bad people, annoying, but not evil. Jake peered at the lit window, uncomfortable, because that meant he couldn't pretend that he was hiding in the shadows out of some noble responsibility to make sure Josie was safe. He couldn't even blame it on his aversion to coming in second. Okay, part of it *might* have been jealousy. Most of it was Josie. That was where it got complicated. He hadn't been able to get her out of his head ever since he'd heard her laugh. For crying out loud, he'd found himself saying her name every time he thought about those hundred acres over by Sugar Creek. It was almost as if someone was tampering with his thoughts.

Catching a movement out of the corner of his eye, he turned his head just as Rory ambled down the steps. He was whistling, but his steps didn't appear any more jaunty than usual. Jake took that as a good sign.

While Rory got in his truck and drove away, Jake tried to decide what to do. *There wouldn't be any harm in sauntering on up to her place and saying hello.* Jake peered around. The voice had been in his head, but it hadn't sounded like his conscience. It was the damnedest thing. But it wasn't a bad idea.

Maybe he and Josie *could* talk awhile. Maybe she would laugh again.

He eased out of the truck, looked all around and set off for the stairs. His tread was light, and a pleasant breeze wafted through his shirt as he raised his fist and knocked softly on the glass.

Josie was smiling when she opened the door. He could hardly blame her smile for slipping away. His arrival *was* a surprise.

"Evening, Josephine."

"Jake!"

He noticed how nice she looked in her light green dress. "Nice night," he said.

"Yes, I guess it is." Her eyes were shining and her lips formed another smile, this one for him. It was amazing, the way she made smiling look so easy. She appeared to have had a good time with Rory. She didn't, however, appear to have been kissed. It was a shame, too, because she had such a kissable mouth.

He would never know what made him swoop down, covering her mouth with his. Her lips parted on a gasp. He brought his hand to her face, threading his fingers through her hair. His mouth moved over hers even as he tipped her head back, deepening the kiss, her surprise slowly turning into pleasure. A soft groan sounded in her throat, and her lips opened beneath his. Lord, she tasted sweet, her lips moist and warm and giving.

Her fingertips fluttered to the back of his hand, brushing his knuckles. Her hand was small, her touch soft, her kiss so heady it was as if something that had been tightly coiled deep inside him was starting to unravel. Ah, Jake thought. He'd been too long without a woman.

Josie knew she should open her eyes, but she lacked the strength. All she could do was strain toward Jake's warmth. One second his kiss was as tender and light as the summer breeze. The next it was deep and searing, lingering, savoring, devouring. She'd been kissed a thousand times, but she'd never been kissed quite like this.

Tom's mouth had always become softer as he'd kissed her. There was nothing soft in this kiss. It was possessive, demanding, the tiniest bit savage. It made her feel naughty, and nice, and young, and free. And very, very single.

Shock ran through her, and she drew back, her eyes finally opening. Jake's fingers were still tangled in her hair, his lips still wet from her kiss, his eyes clouded with passion. Her heart was hammering wildly, foolishly. "Wh-why did you do that?"

He took his time drawing away, letting his fingers comb through her hair. "There are sparks between us."

"Spar—Jake," she said, feeling guilty. "What are you doing here?"

She'd called him Jake. She hadn't intended to, but it had just slipped out. After that kiss, she didn't see how she would be able to call him *Mr.* McKenna again.

While she was trying to regain her equilibrium, his gaze probed hers, then strayed to her mouth. "I didn't plan this. The kiss, I mean. I wanted to see you, talk to you. May I come in, Josephine?"

She was feeling a little off-kilter and thought about telling him it was late. She was tired. But then she caught sight of his expression, at his lips that seemed so unaccustomed to smiling and the crease in one lean cheek, and she didn't have the heart to turn him away. Drawing in a shaky breath, she gestured him inside.

It was very gentlemanly of him to remove his hat, but she thought it was at odds with the man, because there was nothing gentle about Jake McKenna. Not the way he looked, not the way he moved, certainly not the way he'd kissed her. He wasn't like any other man she'd ever met.

"You wanted to talk to me?" she asked, averting her gaze.

"I find myself in a very precarious situation," he said quietly.

She took a deep breath and let it all out. "Precarious situations are best discussed sitting down." Moving past him, she led the way to the sofa.

He lowered his frame into a threadbare, but cozy, overstuffed chair she'd picked up for a song when she'd first moved to South Dakota. It looked smaller with him in it. Her entire apartment *felt* smaller with him in it. She tried to figure out why. He was tall, yes, but no seven-footer. His shoulders were broad, yet he was lean, his waist narrow, his arms and legs muscular. Her gaze strayed to his hands. Forget faces or physiques. It was a man's hands she always paid attention to the most. After all, it was a man's hands that put out fires, swung a hammer, wielded a rope, stroked a woman's body.

And Jake McKenna had the most amazing hands. They

were work roughened, right down to the tips of his long, slightly crooked fingers. There was strength in those hands. She wondered if there was gentleness, too.

Forget it, she told herself. She didn't need to know why he made her apartment seem smaller. She had to put an end to this breathlessness, this feeling of wonder. She would hear Jake out, and then she would send him on his way.

"Does this have anything to do with the reading of your father's will?" she asked.

His chin moved only a fraction of an inch. It was enough to alert her to his surprise.

"What do you know about my father's will?"

There was no getting around the sharp edge in his voice or the ice in his glare. If Josie were able to see auras, she was sure his would have just changed colors. She slipped out of her shoes and drew her legs up, tucking her feet under her dress. "Rory mentioned a certain stipulation."

"O'Grady talked to you about this?"

"He mentioned that one of his cowhands happened to hear about it."

Jake sprang to his feet. "*Happened* to hear it, my—eye. That cowboy might as well have bugged my barn."

"It's all right, Jake. Rory swore the other man to silence."

Jake forced himself to take a calming breath. Rory had found out about that stipulation, and he'd told Josie about it. Jake didn't know what Rory had up his sleeve, but it was up to Jake to salvage what he could. Since there was no use beating around the bush, he sat back down and laid his cards on the table. Steepling his fingers beneath his chin, he looked at Josie. "Did Rory explain that, in order to keep my land, I must be a married man by July?" He held her gaze for several seconds. When she shook her head he said, "I need a wife, Josie, and I need one soon."

Josie made herself more comfortable in the corner of her sofa. She thought it was too bad there were so few women in Jasper Gulch. It made things difficult for all the men in the area. It made things especially difficult for a man who'd just admitted that he needed a wife, and soon. Aware of the silence filling the room, she glanced sideways at Jake. He was watching her, waiting in silent expectation.

"I wouldn't expect to get something for nothing," he said.

She smiled, closed her eyes, relaxing by degrees. "Of course you wouldn't, Jake."

He cleared his throat. "I'm willing to make it worth your while."

"You're willing to make it worth my— Are you telling me you want *me* to marry you?"

He nodded.

"Why me?"

"Who else is there?" Jake's lips thinned, and he nearly blanched. Damn, he hadn't intended to let that slip.

She lifted her hair away from her nape, letting the loose tendrils topple down her back once again. There was something about the way she tipped her head back and closed her eyes, something feminine and appealing and arousing. For a moment he forgot why he was there. "I didn't mean that the way it sounded," he said quietly.

"Don't worry, Jake. I acquired a thick skin a long time ago. I heard through the Jasper Gulch grapevine that you paid a little visit to Crystal Galloway. I'm assuming she turned you down?"

It struck him that Josie wasn't upset by his businesslike proposal. She didn't even seem to be angry about the woman who was ahead of her on his list. It rankled. A woman, no matter how plain, should expect a man who was proposing to treat her as if she were the only woman in the world.

"Mama," a small voice called before Jake had answered Josie's question. "I'm thirsty."

Josie rose to her feet instantly. "I'll be right back."

It was a relief to put a little distance between her and Jake. There was just something about him that left her feeling unsettled. She didn't know how he did it, but he rattled her. It was more than that kiss. It was…everything. It was Jake.

She made a quick stop in the bathroom for a glass and some water. Slipping into Kelsey's tiny room, she said, "Here ya go, sweet pea."

Kelsey barely took a sip from the glass. "What's that nice Mr. McKenna doing here, Mama?"

Jake McKenna, nice? "He just stopped in to say hello." Now, to change to subject. "Did you and Savannah eat owl pills?" she asked around a smile. Kelsey was rarely wide-awake this time of night. "Do you want another drink of water?"

Kelsey was so intent upon asking questions, she seemed to have completely forgotten about her ruse to lure Josie into her room. She didn't even bother shaking her head. Instead, she pushed the glass away and asked, "Do you like him, Mama?"

"I like most everyone," Josie said, hedging.

Kelsey rolled her eyes expressively. "Do you like Rory better?"

Josie considered the question. Rory was easier to be with, laugh with, talk with. But easier to like? "Go to sleep now."

"But Mama, I hafta know."

Kelsey's theatrics were amazing. Josie had a feeling she

was going to be in big trouble when her daughter hit puberty. "You have to know tonight?" she whispered.

The imp nodded vehemently.

"I like them both, Kelsey, but..."

"Haley says you've gotta be in love before I can get a new daddy. Do you think you could love one of them by the last day of school?"

So that was what this was all about. Josie placed the glass of water on the nightstand and smoothed the baby-fine hair away from her daughter's face. Kelsey had been four years old when Tom had died. Now, two years later, her memories of her father were vague at best. In some ways, Josie thought it was a blessing, because her little girl couldn't miss somebody she couldn't remember. But then Haley Carson, an older girl Kelsey met at school, had mentioned the annual family fun day that was held the last day of school each year, and how she and her father had won the three-legged race last year. Kelsey had been adamant about finding a new father ever since.

"Couldn't you just try to love one of them, please?"

It made Josie feel sad, because she couldn't give her little girl everything she wanted and needed. She tried to tell herself no parent could. "I love you enough for a hundred people, sweet pea."

"I love you, too, Mama."

Kelsey's sigh tugged on Josie's heart strings and made her yearn to be everything to her child. "I'll go with you on the last day of school."

The little girl sighed again and quietly closed her eyes. Josie wondered if all mothers felt so inadequate and so full of love at the same time. If only Tom hadn't died.

But he had, Josie told herself as she returned the glass to the bathroom. She stifled a yawn. Feeling blue, she assured herself she was just tired. She'd received two marriage proposals in one night from two different men, neither of whom so much as pretended to love her. No wonder she felt done in.

Kelsey was happy, most of the time. As long as it was truly what she needed, there wasn't anything Josie wouldn't do for her child. But she couldn't marry a man she didn't love just so Kelsey had two parents to bring to the fun day at school.

Give the man a chance.

She smiled just as she always did when she heard Tom's voice. Meeting her own gaze in the mirror, she whispered, "Which man, Tom? Rory or Jake?"

Her mind filled only with the sound of silence.

She pushed her hair away from her forehead and did an about-face, grumbling to herself that men who were angels answered questions about as well as husbands who were still human.

"Did you say something?"

Jake's voice brought her out of her reverie. Pausing in the doorway, she said, "I guess I was talking to myself."

"Is she okay?"

Josie almost said, "Who?" Luckily she caught herself before she could embarrass herself further. For heaven's sake, what was wrong with her?

"Kelsey's fine. She's just a little wound up after spending the evening with her friend, Savannah Colter."

Jake glanced from the woman in the photograph he'd been studying to the woman standing across the room. In the picture, Josie was laughing up at a young man who was laughing in return. It was an action shot, slightly out of focus, and had probably been taken with a cheap camera. The playfulness and happiness came through as clear as day. In comparison the woman across the room looked tired and pale.

"Is this your late husband?"

She strolled to him, turning his hand so she could see the photograph in the frame. "That's him. Thomas Callahan. The big lug."

Jake followed the course of her gaze to the ceiling. Other than a yellow water spot where the roof had leaked at one time or another, there was nothing to see.

She turned her attention to the photograph and so did Jake. "He was twenty when we got married. I was nineteen. His parents had big plans for their only child. I was poor. Trailer trash, they called me. Tom happened to overhear. His mother tried to cover up, but his father came right out and told Tom he was making the mistake of a lifetime. 'Go ahead and bed her,' he said. 'But for God's sake, don't marry her.' Tom told his father he loved me, and if they couldn't accept that, they no longer had a son. It was the only time I ever heard him raise his voice."

Jake studied Josie's face. She was staring at the collar on his shirt, but he doubted it was what she was seeing. Her innermost feelings played across her features. Pride, fatigue, sadness. She'd loved the man in the picture. Jake wondered what it would feel like to be loved like that. Longing stretched over him, until it became all but impossible to fight his growing need to touch her. He almost reached for her hand, and Jake McKenna never reached for anyone.

"How did he die?" he asked quietly.

Her throat convulsed on a swallow, her eyes coming into focus. "We thought he had the flu. It was going around, but then, isn't it always? Looking back, I should have known. But at the time I just never imagined he might be seriously, gravely ill. He had a headache, and he was weak. When he got worse instead of better, we went to the doctor. By then a week had gone by, and Tom was starting to babble, and it was hard for him to walk. The doctor took one look at him and put him right in the hospital for tests. Tom went into a coma later that night. He had brain cancer. People told us at the time it was a blessing that we hadn't known, because it was incurable, fast growing and inoperable. At least Tom never had to deal with knowing he was going to die. But he never made amends with his parents, either. He died two days later. He was twenty-five.''

Her voice had dipped so low Jake could practically feel it brushing across the toes of his boots. Her husband had been young. Too young to die. She'd been young, too. She'd already had her fill of bad luck and bad news, of heartache and difficult decisions. No wonder she hadn't jumped at the chance to marry *him*. No matter how badly he needed to find a wife, she would be better off without his problems.

He took a backward step. "It's time I was going." He didn't wait for her to say anything. Retrieving his hat on his way past the table, he crammed it on his head, opened the door, and walked through.

"What will you do?" she asked.

He was halfway down the stairs when he glanced up at her, longing stretching over him again. "Do?" he asked.

"About your land."

He gave himself a mental shake and a mental kick. He really had been too long without a woman. "I honestly don't know. But it's not your concern."

"I, er, that is, I've been wanting to see the countryside. I hear the pasqueflower is in bloom."

They stood watching each other, neither speaking. Jake hadn't noticed any flowers in bloom. But then, he rarely did. He knew a hint when he heard one, though. If he hadn't seen the photograph of Josie and her husband, he would have seized the opportunity she was offering him. But he'd seen the love shining in her eyes for her dead husband, heard it in her voice.

He had to get out of there.

"If you leak that to the Jasper Gulch grapevine," he said, "there'll be fifty single men who are willing to show you the countryside lining up at your doorstep in no time at all. You'll have to let me know how it turns out. Good night, Josephine."

"I...you..." Her voice trailed away, only to resume with renewed vehemence. "Why, of all the nerve! I'll have you know I'm not a charity case. I don't want fifty men lining up on my doorstep, and I wouldn't spend the day with you, Jake McKenna, if you were the last man on earth."

It occurred to him as he stared at the color on her cheeks and the anger in her eyes, that she hadn't answered his question regarding his marriage proposal. All in all he thought the loud slam of the door was a pretty good indication that the conversation had ended.

That, he thought to himself as he made his way to his truck, was why he didn't make a habit of being kind. Chivalry was dead, they said. There was a good reason for that. A very good reason, indeed.

Chapter Three

"**Y**ou went and made her mad?" Slappy Purvis griped. "Why on earth would you go and do a fool thing like that?"

"Yeah, Jake," Buck Matthews grumbled around the cigarette he'd just lit. "I could'a given you a few pointers. All you had to do was ask."

Teeth clenched, Jake surveyed a section of fence the herd had taken out the night before and did his best to ignore his hired hands. They didn't seem to notice.

Slappy was close to sixty, but Buck and Billy were both in their early twenties. All three were single, got along better with horses than with people and had manners that needed work. If they *had* given him advice, Jake would have been hard-pressed to take it.

Buck scratched at his three-day beard. "The moon was full last night. It would'a been easy for a coyote or a wolf to see. Could be that's what spooked the herd. Still, I always figured a full moon was a good time to kiss a gal, not make her mad."

"Me, too," Billy Schmidt, the youngest of the hired hands declared. "Kissin' 'em is a lot more fun than fightin' with 'em."

"Maybe Jake here don't see it that way," Slappy grumbled. "Either that or he kissed her first and made her mad second."

Three pairs of eyes were suddenly on Jake. "Did you?" Billy asked. "Did you kiss her first?"

Jake clenched his teeth a little tighter. Somebody from the Crazy Horse had seen him leaving Josie's place last night, but as far as he knew, his ranch hands weren't aware of the stipulation in his father's will. Which meant that their curiosity was coming from a male perspective, not worry about McKenna land.

Holding a board in place with his shoulder, he eyed his men. "Were you boys planning to earn your pay today?"

Slappy let out a snort that rivaled his horse's. "We earn our pay every day. Oh, oh. You're gettin' that look on your face. You know, the one old Isaac wore most of the time. Now, before you go gettin' all riled, I know how much you balk at the idea that you're anything like your old man. If you ain't careful, you're gonna end up just like him. I'm afraid it takes a woman to bring out the best in most men. Which is why me and the boys are so interested in knowin' what was all said betweenst you and the widow Callahan."

Jake wrapped new wire around the board he'd replaced, but he didn't reply. His expression must have been telling, because Billy grinned. "I knew it. He kissed her. Hey, Sky, get over here. Jake's gonna tell us how he kissed Josie Callahan."

Sky dropped an armful of lumber before sauntering toward them. "Come on boys," he said, his lope easy, his expression friendly. "Leave the boss alone and get to work."

That, Jake thought, as Buck, Slappy and Billy tramped over to a nearby section of fence, sputtering all the while, was why Skyler Buchanan was his right-hand man. The two of them went back a long way. Sky might have taken chances Jake didn't approve of, and he offered advice when Jake didn't want any, but he never so much as implied that Jake was anything like his old man. Jake was nothing like his mother, either. He was thankful for small favors. Nadine McKenna had left Isaac and her only two sons for a man who'd made it big in the oil fields down in Texas. She'd sent presents at Christmas and had visited him and his brother a few times at first. The last time she'd come home had been after Cole had died. Her tears had seemed real enough, but Jake hadn't been fooled.

She'd begged him not to hate her. Jake didn't hate her. He wasn't sure if he'd loved her by then, though. She was his *mother*. *She* was supposed to love *him*. She sure as hell wasn't supposed to bustle right back to her rich Texan and leave her only surviving son with a man like Isaac McKenna. A man who pushed and pushed for the best and who never gave credit where credit was due. A man who didn't like many people, not even his second son. Jake had tried at first. After a while he'd figured out that it didn't matter how hard he tried. He would never be able to take the place of Isaac's *firstborn*.

Jake had never blamed Isaac for loving Cole. Jake had loved his older brother, too. The thing he remembered the most about his mother's leaving was how quiet the house was after she was gone. It was nothing compared to how quiet it got after Cole died. Looking back, Jake wondered how he'd survived the rest of his childhood. The days had been lifeless and silent, the nights worse. And then one afternoon, the summer he turned seventeen, Skyler Buchanan drove up the driveway in a noisy, rusty pickup truck. He needed work, he'd said, and a roof over his head. Isaac had hired him on the spot, and the ranch hadn't been quiet since.

"I talked to Boomer Brown a little while ago," Jake told Sky. "He says he has some lumber he can spare. How's the fence look down that way?"

Sky moved a blade of prairie grass from one side of his mouth to the other. "Not as bad as this section, but it's still gonna have to be reinforced. So, was she a good kisser?"

Jake shot Sky a silencing look. Sky's grin broadened. "Well?"

"I suppose."

"If you tried really hard, McKenna, you might be able to work your way up to vague. *I suppose* doesn't tell us a whole helluva lot, does it, boys?"

Billy, Buck and Slappy shook their heads from their positions several feet away.

"I kissed her. There. Are you satisfied?"

"The question is," Sky said, "are you?"

Buck, Slappy and Billy all raised their eyebrows in silent expectation. Jake recalled the way Josie's voice had risen when she'd told him she wouldn't spend the day with him if he were the last man on earth. *That* hadn't been particularly satisfying. With a scowl hot enough to scorch the rich prairie grass, he turned on his heel.

"Where are you going?" Sky called to his back.

"To Boomer's to get that lumber. In case you haven't noticed, we have fences to mend."

Jake was too far away to hear Sky's reply, but in his head, a voice whispered, *There's more than one kind of fence in need of mending today, my friend.*

That voice. It was driving Jake crazy. What did it mean *friend?* He'd never considered his conscience his friend.

Cussing under his breath, he climbed into his truck and sped down the lane.

"How long before we get there, Mama?"

Hoping Kelsey didn't notice how tightly her mother was clutching the steering wheel, Josie answered in the middle of the invocations and supplications she'd been reciting to herself since she'd first noticed the engine light come on a couple of miles back. "Ten more miles, sweet pea, and we'll be home."

Please, she begged just in case there was a patron saint of engines. Just hold on for ten more miles. The car sputtered. Josie gripped the steering wheel even tighter.

Something popped. Josie jumped. There was a hiss, and then steam poured out from under the hood, spewing and writhing and roiling upward until Josie couldn't see.

Dread wrapped around her windpipe, squeezing like a fist. Heaving a huge sigh, she coasted to the side of the road and turned off the engine.

"What's the matter, Mama? Why is the car smoking?"

"I don't know, Kelsey. Something must have overheated."

Josie had seen vehicles in similar situations sitting along highways, hoods up, engines steaming, drivers shaking their heads forlornly.

Kelsey unhooked her seat belt and pressed her little face close to the windshield. "What are we gonna do?"

Do? Josie didn't know. She had insurance, but not road service. That took money, and she was fresh out of that. She'd been relying on luck. It seemed she was fresh out of that, as well.

She always closed the store early on Wednesdays. Today all she'd wanted to do was take a leisurely drive with her little girl. Back in Mississippi, people went mushrooming this time of year. She and Kelsey hadn't spotted any mush-rooms, but they had discovered a vast array of wildflowers swaying in the never-ending breeze. Kelsey wanted to take them to school for show and tell the following day. They'd checked out a book about wildflowers from the library. So far Kelsey had identified every type of flower she'd found. Up until now the excursion had been fun, and it had been free. Free was good. A broken-down car wasn't.

Josie glanced at the clouds that seemed to be pressing down on the earth from every direction. If they'd been closer to town there would have been farmhouses nearby. She tried to remember how far it was to the nearest house out here. One mile? Three? She hoped to high heaven it wasn't farther than that.

"It looks like we're going to have to walk, sweet pea."

Kelsey's calm acceptance sent a lump to Josie's throat. Her little girl was a real trooper.

"Can you carry my book, Mama?"

Josie reached for the library book while Kelsey reached for the flowers she'd picked. Hand in hand, mother and daughter started down the road. Before long Kelsey was singing "Old McDonald," and Josie was joining in.

Ten minutes into the trek, the little trooper was tired of singing. She was tired of walking. She was just plain tired and hungry and whiny. Fifteen minutes into the walk, it started to rain. Josie wanted to cry. Instead she started sing-ing "Itsy Bitsy Spider."

Kelsey was no longer in the mood to sing and wanted to be carried. Hiking her child onto her back, Josie thought things couldn't get any worse.

A few minutes later she heard the rumble of an engine in the distance behind them. There, see? she told herself. Help was on the way. Squinting through the rain, she could make out the shape of a pickup truck speeding toward them. It was a black pickup truck. Why, it looked like—

Her heart fell. It seemed that things could always get worse.

Within seconds the truck pulled to a stop beside her. She tried to take a deep breath for courage. It wasn't easy, what with the stranglehold Kelsey had around her neck and the way Jake McKenna was staring directly at her through the open passenger window.

"Hi, Mr. McKenna," Kelsey quipped from Josie's back. "Mama's car broked down."

Jake flicked the girl a quick glance, his gaze once again probing Josie's. "Get in."

Josie licked fresh rainwater from her lips. "I hate to trouble you."

"Get in."

Sighing, Josie didn't see what choice she had. She lowered Kelsey to the ground, reached for her daughter's hand and opened the door.

Sitting in the seat between the adults, Kelsey didn't seem to notice the tense atmosphere inside the truck. "See this flower?" she said, holding her bouquet toward Jake. "It's a pasqueflower. Mama says it's South Dakota's state flower. It's pretty, isn't it?"

Josie recalled telling Jake that she would like to see the countryside with him. He'd turned down her request, which had sparked her temper and had caused her to say something that hadn't been very nice. Her cheeks grew warm despite the chill in the air. Oh, but that redhead's temper of hers was going to be the death of her yet.

Wiping the cover of the library book on the skirt of her damp dress, she peered at the sky that was as dull and gray as the day. "I didn't know it was going to rain. I would be very grateful if you could give us a ride back to town. I'll reimburse you for gas as soon as I can."

He grunted an answer Josie couldn't quite hear.

"Mrs. Carson likes the rain, Mama. She says it's just as important as the sun. Look," Kelsey said, pointing. "A river."

Josie sat up a little straighter. They hadn't crossed a river on their way out to the country. Eyeing the unfamiliar road, she said, "This isn't the way back to town."

"The Lone M is closer. And this isn't a river. It's Sugar Creek."

Kelsey craned her head so she could see out Jake's window. "Why do they call it Sugar Creek? I don't see no sugar."

"I don't see *any* sugar," Josie corrected.

"Me, neither," Kelsey replied.

Steering around a huge pothole in the road, Jake said, "It isn't always sugar that makes something sweet. There are dozens of creeks in South Dakota. Plum Creek, Bear in the Lodge Creek, and Wounded Knee Creek. There's Horsehead Creek, Cheery Creek and Turtle Creek, but Sugar Creek is the only one in this part of the state. In late summer, water is sweeter than sugar, and Sugar Creek carries the sweetest water of all."

Jake could feel the little girl's gaze on him. Glancing down, he saw intelligence in those dark brown eyes. For someone so small, she seemed to have an uncanny ability to comprehend. He half expected her to say something profound.

She raised her chin a notch, skewed her little mouth to one side and finally said, "How come you call a crick a creek?"

Jake blinked. And then he did something he hadn't done in a long, long time. He laughed.

Josie couldn't help staring at Jake's profile. His laughter sounded a little like an engine that was having trouble turning over, but it eased the taut lines beside his mouth and eliminated some of the tension inside the cab of his truck. She wondered what it would take to ease the tension completely.

Smoothing a hand over Kelsey's wet hair, she said, "Back in Mississippi, we pronounced creek 'crick.'" She glanced sideways at Jake. "Mississippians are noted for being easy to amuse but hard to convince."

"I've noticed."

Their gazes caught, held.

The moment might have gone on forever, if Jake hadn't felt a tug on his sleeve a moment before the little girl said, "How old are you, Mr. McKenna?"

A quick glance was all it took to let him know the child was peering up at him. Only his seventh-grade teacher had ever studied him so long or so hard. "I'm thirty-two."

"Is that too old, Mama?"

Before Josie could answer, Kelsey said, "My daddy's in heaven."

"Yes," he said, "I know."

"I need another one."

Josie gasped. "Kelsey, please."

Kelsey shrugged off her mother's hand. "Daddy's gonna help find me one."

"I beg your pardon?" Jake asked as he turned into the Lone M's driveway.

"It's nothing," Josie said.

"My daddy," Kelsey insisted. "He's gonna help Mama find a husbun' and me a daddy. He told Mama so. Mama says she don't want another husbun' on accounta she still loves Daddy. But he says it's time to go on. Tell him, Mama."

Tell him? Josie thought, mortified. She couldn't think, let alone speak. It didn't matter, because before her eyes, the shutters closed over Jake's entire expression.

He pulled to a stop near a big white house, opened his door and got out. Josie and Kelsey climbed out from the other side just as two young cowboys ambled down the porch steps, rain running off their tattered Stetsons. One of them eyed Josie. The other eyed the empty bed of Jake's truck. "Now that," the second one said to the first, "is why Jake's the boss."

"Yeah," the first one said. "Only Jake could leave to get lumber and come back with a woman."

Josie liked the cowhands immediately, but Jake didn't so much as crack a smile. "Buck, Billy," he said. "Josie's car quit over on Shavey Road just past Old Stump Road. It looks like the radiator overheated. Check it out. Take some water and radiator fluid with you. Bring the car back here when you're through."

"That isn't necessary," Josie said as soon as she and Kelsey were safely out of the rain on the porch. Glancing from Jake to the other men, she smiled. "If one of you would be so kind as to give me a ride back to town, Kelsey and I will be out of your way."

She caught the looks the cowhands cast their boss. It only took a small movement of Jake's head to spur them into action.

"Come on inside," Jake said, "where it's dry."

Josie considered arguing, but Kelsey shivered. Taking her child's hand, Josie followed Jake into a large foyer. She slipped out of her shoes and helped Kelsey out of hers.

"Mama," Kelsey whispered close to Josie's ear. "I'm hungry."

Jake led the way into a large kitchen where he instructed them to have a seat at the polished table, then disappeared through a doorway on the opposite end of the room. He was back within seconds, a stack of towels in his hand. Thanking him politely, Josie reached for the top one and promptly began drying her daughter's face and hair. The next thing Josie knew, Jake placed a platter of cold chicken in front of them.

Kelsey's eyes grew large, but she held back, waiting for Josie's gentle nod before digging in. While Kelsey ate cold chicken with her fingers, Josie dried her own face and hair, strolling to a wide, arched doorway. She could see the living room from here. There was a stone fireplace on one wall, an open staircase on the other. The house was large and attractive, but it felt cold and empty, and she doubted it was due to the rain. She turned slowly, thinking that it wouldn't take a lot to make the house warm and inviting. She wondered what it would take to warm Jake McKenna.

She looked at him and found him watching her. Her nerves skittered up and down her spine like goose bumps. In an attempt to fill the silence, she said, "Your home is lovely. And very quiet."

A muscle worked in his cheek before he answered. "It was my father's castle. It wasn't always this quiet."

Rubbing her upper arms to warm them, she felt on the verge of knowing him, or at least a part of him he normally kept hidden. With Kelsey smacking her lips in the background, Josie sent him a tentative smile and said, "I'm trying to picture you making a lot of noise."

He strolled closer. "When our father was away, my brother and I used to play cowboys and Indians with a couple of neighbor kids. We'd whoop and holler and slide down the banister only to tear up the stairs and do it all over again."

This was the first Josie had heard any mention of Jake's brother. Curious, she said, "What's your brother's name?"

"Cole. His name was Cole."

His expression changed in the blink of an eye, and a look she recognized too well settled over his face. Josie didn't ask any more questions. She didn't have to. Some people went twenty, thirty, even forty years without a single serious brush with sadness. She'd had an intimate knowledge of it since she was eight years old and her father had died. Ten years later her mother had followed. Both of those losses had left her feeling hollow, but neither of them had rocked her entire world as deeply and completely as Tom's death two years ago. Maybe the reason she'd been able to go on when other women fell completely apart was because she'd had so much practice. Or maybe it was because she'd had no choice. Kelsey had needed her.

Those people who had loved and lost and lived to tell about it had a depth that someone who hadn't grieved didn't always see or understand. Josie called that depth battle scars. Jake's were as deep and jagged as any she'd ever sensed.

"Do you have any other family?" she asked quietly.

"I have the ranch."

It seemed to Josie that a person needed to live for more than land, no matter how big the spread or how rich the soil. But who was she to judge? Breaking eye contact, she glanced at Kelsey. Just looking at her little girl made her heart swell to bursting. "I hope you weren't planning on those leftovers for supper."

Jake shook his head, but it wasn't easy. He had the strangest feeling that he was floating. It had to do with the expression in Josie's eyes and the musical lilt in her voice. He swore he could have gone on listening to her forever.

"Other mothers," she said, as if obliging him, "complain that their children don't eat enough to keep a bird alive. Not Kelsey. She was born ravenous. She inherited her father's appetite.''

Her mention of her late husband brought Jake to his senses much the way a rock found the ground: with a hard thud. All three of them turned at the engine noise in the driveway. Moments later Buck and Billy strolled into the house.

"Your car's up and running," Buck told Josie.

"Jake was right," Billy added. "It just needed radiator fluid. But I checked the oil, too, just to make sure. Near as I can tell, it's in good shape. I parked it in the driveway for you."

"What a relief," she exclaimed. "Thank you both so much."

Both men nodded. After casting a quick glance at Jake, they tugged at the brims of their hats and backed from the room.

Once again the house was quiet.

"Well." Josie cleared her throat. "I guess we'll be going."

As if on cue, Kelsey wiped her hands on a paper napkin and slid from her chair. "Thanks, Mr. McKenna."

Josie said, "Yes, thanks. For everything."

"No problem."

"I mean it," she continued. "Thank you for offering Kelsey a snack and for coming to our rescue. It was very noble of you."

Jake blinked. Noble? Him? That was a new one. He would have to try not to let it happen again.

He felt a tug on his shirt. Head tipped way back, Kelsey looked up at him in silent expectation. It took him a few seconds to realize she wanted him to bend down to her level. He'd had little experience with children, none whatsoever with skinny waifs with appetites like their fathers'.

He hunkered down and met this waif's stare. She smelled like cold fried chicken and rain, and she looked at him with eyes that made him feel things he didn't necessarily want to feel. Just when he thought she was never going to do or say anything, she held out her hand and whispered, "These are for you."

He never saw the kiss on his cheek coming. His breath stuck in his throat, and his heart chugged as if it had just brushed an electric fence. By the time his legs were fully operational and he could stand, Kelsey had twirled around, and she and her mother were gone.

Jake stood at the window for a long time, his heart beating a slow rhythm, a bouquet of wildflowers clutched tight in his left hand.

Josie sat at her kitchen table, adding up numbers, jotting down amounts, figuring and refiguring until the columns swam before her eyes. It was no use. She was going to have to close her store and find a paying job. She'd feared it a month ago, had known it a week ago. It was time to face it once and for all. It was the only solution to her financial difficulties.

It wasn't the end of the world. It had been a long day, a long week, a long year, that was all. But tomorrow was another day. It would be a better one.

"Isn't that right, Tom?" she said a short time later as she was getting ready for bed. She listened with all her might. Tom was either in no mood to answer, or else he was visiting with some other spirit friend of his over on Mars or something. Sure, Josie thought as she got ready for bed. Now he wouldn't answer. A few weeks ago she couldn't get him to shut up.

Her mind began to wander as she brushed her teeth. She'd gone through the Help Wanted ads in the newspapers earlier. Pierre wasn't exactly a hopping metropolis, but surely, somebody somewhere needed a clerk or a typist, a grocery store checker or a waitress. She planned to drive to Pierre as soon as she got Kelsey off to school in the morning.

It was lucky for her Jake's ranch hands had gotten her car running. The mere thought of Jake, no matter how fleeting, brought his image into sharp focus in her mind. She could see his expression so clearly, could remember with such clarity the deep undertones in his voice when he'd told her his brother's name had been Cole. His voice had been much more clipped a few days earlier when he'd said he needed a wife. Jake McKenna was a very complex man. As she crawled into bed, it occurred to her that he needed a wife, but not for the reason he'd mentioned. Not to keep his land, but to reach his heart.

She switched off the lamp and shook away the notion. She was having enough trouble keeping her head above water these days. She'd wanted to curl up and die right along with Tom, but she'd had Kelsey to think about and to love. In many ways she'd lived for her child. She wondered what Jake really lived for.

"Is land enough for a man to live for, Tom?" she whispered.

She squeezed her eyes shut and listened with all her might. The only sound she heard was the sigh of the wind after midnight. Flopping onto her back, she stared at the dark ceiling. Fine, she thought. Don't answer. She didn't need to understand what went on in the deepest recesses of Jake McKenna's mind, anyway. It wasn't as if she planned to marry him. She didn't want to marry anybody.

"Did you hear that, you big lug?"

Who are you calling a lug?

The grin spreading across Josie's face didn't stop until

it reached her heart. Pulling the blankets up to her chin, she closed her eyes. Tomorrow she would look for a job. Mmm. She snuggled into her pillow. Yes, tomorrow would be a better day.

But the next morning Josie wasn't so sure about that. Kelsey had gotten up on the wrong side of bed and hadn't wanted to wear anything in her closet. She'd gone to school looking forlorn and bedraggled in a faded yellow jumper and her holey shoes. Josie couldn't even smile at the double entendre. Holy shoes. There was nothing holy about trying to explain to her little girl why she had to wait to have a new pair of cheap tennis shoes. Plus, it was still raining. To top it all off, Josie hadn't had one customer. For a day that was supposed to be better than the last one, it had started off mighty dismal.

She was in the back room when she heard the bell jingle over the door. Voilà! a customer. Just like that, her gloom receded. She pushed through the curtained doorway and came face-to-face with a man wearing a uniform. "Can I help you?" she asked.

"I'm looking for Josephine Callahan."

"I'm Josie Callahan."

Her smile slid away when the young man handed her a letter. "Please sign here."

With trepidation prickling up and down her spine, she scribbled her name. "Is something wrong?"

The man shrugged. "I don't know. I'm only the messenger."

A moment later the bell jingled again, signaling the deliveryman's departure. Turning her back on her store, she studied the official-looking envelope in her hand. Her fingers shook as she tore the letter open. She stared at the letter, worry and dread fighting for equal space in the pit of her stomach. Halfway into the letter, she slumped into a chair. Eyes closed, she brought her hand to her throat. The letter was from Tom's parents, more specifically, from their attorney.

They understood how difficult the past two years had been for her, the letter stated. They knew about her financial situation. Josie wondered how they'd found out. She certainly hadn't gone to them for help with Tom's hospital or funeral expenses.

They wanted to help, the letter said. They knew what a huge undertaking raising a child could be, and they were extending their warmest regards along with a plea that Josie allow them to give Kelsey a more stable environment.

Realization and fear clawed at Josie, making it difficult to breathe. Tom's parents wanted Kelsey, and they were going to try to take her.

Josie swallowed. A tear trailed down her cheek. As another followed, she jerked to her feet and swiped the tears away.

Charles Callahan's most hateful and hurtful words whispered through her mind. "Go ahead and bed her, but don't wed her."

"Oh, Tom," she whispered. "What am I going to do? They don't want to help me. They want to hurt me. They don't care about me or Kelsey. If they did, they'd never try to separate us. They're offering to give me five thousand dollars to make a new start. Five thousand dollars in return for our little girl."

Panic rose up in her throat. She wanted to burn the letter. No. She wanted to take it to an attorney. She read the last paragraph over and over again. She could take it to an attorney, but she doubted it would do any good. Unless she agreed to their terms, they were going to petition for custody of their only grandchild. It was a bribe and a threat,

carefully worded to be legal, but a bribe and a threat none-
theless.

Josie tried to think.

She traipsed into the back room, only to burst through
the curtain seconds later. She paced to the window next.
She caught a glimpse of Rory O'Grady across the street.
He was with Tracy Gentry, and he was flirting up a storm.

Oh, Tom. What am I going to do?

Maybe she should take Kelsey and run away. But where?
She had no money. And Tom's parents had more than they
could spend. Surely they would find her. What then?

Heart racing, she turned in a complete circle. She had
rent, responsibilities, debts to repay. She couldn't run away.
But she couldn't think here, either. Grabbing her drab
brown coat and her umbrella with its bent wire, she pushed
through the door.

She walked to the little cemetery on the outskirts of Jasper Gulch. After strolling along the curving path, past
markers bearing names and dates of people who had lived
and died more than a hundred years ago, she felt more
calm.

The rain was little more than a drizzle now, and Josie's
breathing was under control. She would handle this, just as
she'd handled Tom's death and the past two years without
him.

Yes, she thought, taking a path where the stones dated
back forty or fifty years, she could handle this. She just
wasn't sure how.

By the time she'd reached the center of the quiet cemetery, she'd considered her options. She didn't have many,
but she couldn't give up Kelsey. Not to anybody, but especially not to those coldhearted people who had so cal-
lously turned their backs on their only son.

She'd planned to get a job and slowly pay off her debts.

She needed more than that now. A few days ago she'd received two marriage proposals. For Kelsey's sake, she was going to have to choose one of them. But which one? The man who was charming but would grow bored with her within a month? Or the man who rarely laughed and didn't seem to have a heart?

Which one? she whispered to herself.

A sign? Is that what you said, Tom? I'm to watch for a sign?

She looked all around her, but saw only urns of flowers and flags and a sky gray with rain. With a heavy heart she made her way along the curving path. A movement up ahead drew her attention. She stopped near a maple tree and held perfectly still.

A lone figure in a black Stetson stood on a slight knoll. His back was to her, but it didn't matter. She recognized the broad shoulders and severe posture and the dark hair that trailed past the collar of that faded denim jacket.

Jake McKenna leaned down. From this distance she couldn't see what he was doing, but she didn't think she'd ever seen a lonelier looking man. Reluctant to intrude, she waited until he left by another route. Legs shaking, she walked to the place he had been.

A lump rose to her throat as she read the name on the stone marker. Cole Isaac McKenna. His brother's grave. A sob lodged in her chest as she gazed at the dates on that stone. Today would have been Cole's birthday. He would have been thirty-six years old, but hadn't lived much past sixteen. He'd been gone a long time, but Jake hadn't forgotten.

It seemed that Jake McKenna had a heart after all.

The rain had stopped, and a wan shaft of sunlight filtered through a gap in the clouds, touching upon Kelsey's pasqueflowers resting on the damp ground. Josie stared at those flowers for a long time.

Heaven help her, she had her sign.

She practically ran all the way back to her store. She planned to call Jake and casually invite him over later that evening. But as she watched the second hand slowly make its way around the clock, she thought she was going to climb out of her skin.

She couldn't relax. And she couldn't wait.

She put the Closed sign in the window. Upstairs in her apartment she took a quick shower. Less than an hour later she was standing on Jake's front porch.

Wearing her prettiest dress, her hair loose and wavy around her shoulders, she raised a shaking fist and knocked on his door. She listened for the sound of footsteps inside. Scrunching her dress in her fists, she thought her stomach was going to pitch.

What was she doing? she nearly cried out loud.

She needed to think this through. She couldn't...

But if she didn't...

The door opened just as she was turning to flee. She didn't remember turning around again, but she must have, because she found herself face-to-face with Jake McKenna.

He stood in the doorway, his gaze steady, watchful.

"The answer is yes," she blurted out.

His eyebrows rose fractionally. He didn't smile, but she hadn't expected him to. Stepping onto the porch, he said, "What was the question?"

She swallowed the brand-new lump in her throat, raised her chin and whispered, "Will I marry you?"

Chapter Four

Everything was quiet—the horses, the cattle, the wind, even Jake. Especially Jake. Outwardly Josie held perfectly still, too, but inside, her heart was racing and her breathing was ragged.

There. She'd done it. She'd told Jake she would marry him.

Staring at him across the wide porch, she thought it was nice of him to try to hide his amazement and surprise. Quite a feat for a man people claimed was rarely nice. No matter how others saw him, it had been nice of him to come to her and Kelsey's rescue yesterday. It would be even nicer if he would answer, or at least give her some small indication that he was considering her backward proposal.

Somewhere a cow mooed. Another took up the call. "Jake?" she asked, glancing nervously around. "If you're thinking about saying something, maybe you should do it pretty soon. The desire to run is hitting me hard and fast."

Jake's mind cleared, along with his vision. There Josie was, standing on his front porch in the gray light of a cloudy afternoon, a sudden gust of wind toying with her hair, wrapping her flowered, dime-store dress around her legs. Meeting her gaze, he said, "Hard and fast should never be used in the same sentence."

Her mouth opened on a gasp, and Jake had a strong compulsion to smile. He had an even stronger compulsion to wrap his arms around her and drag her against his body. She peered at him through the tendrils of hair blowing into her eyes, looking for all the world as if she might take flight at any moment. Glancing at the goose bumps on her thin arms, he said, "I think you'd better come in."

He held the door for her, then stood back while she entered. She strolled to the center of the living room while he strode to the fireplace. "I take it you've changed your mind about marrying me," he said quietly.

Her initial answer was a small shrug and an even smaller nod. "Uh-huh," she reiterated. "I mean, yes. That is, you do still need a wife in order to keep your land, don't you?"

"I still need a wife, Josie."

Her hand fluttered to her throat. "Thank God."

The stone fireplace felt cool beneath Jake's shoulder. In comparison, the flush climbing up Josie's neck looked red-hot.

"I didn't mean that the way it sounded," she whispered.

Jake took a moment to study the woman who had just agreed to marry him. Her hair was windblown, her face clean scrubbed and youthful. Beneath the dime-store dress, she was slender, agile, strong. He sensed she wasn't a woman who was accustomed to asking for help. He knew the feeling. Yearning washed over him. Since he knew better than to allow himself to be distracted by romantic notions, he concentrated on the way he was responding physically and pretended he didn't notice the inkling of hope that seemed to have found its way into his chest.

He strolled a few steps in her direction before planting his feet a comfortable distance apart and crossing his arms at his chest. "There's no need to be nervous, Josie."

She glanced at the open staircase, then slowly reached into her pocket. Drawing out an official-looking envelope, she said, "Believe me, there are plenty of reasons to be nervous. You've entrusted me with your secret. It's only fair that I entrust you with mine."

Her fingers shook as she handed him the letter. Without a word he removed a crisp sheet of paper from the envelope, unfolded it and began to read. He skimmed the first paragraph, something restless and unwelcome stirring inside him, squeezing out his wistfulness. After carefully reading the final paragraph, he looked at Josie. "Hell of a couple, your in-laws."

She nodded only once. "What do you think?"

He stuffed the letter back into its envelope. What did he think? He thought he should have been happier with this new turn of events. Maybe he didn't know how to be happy anymore. Maybe he never had.

He handed her the letter but didn't readily release it, so that the tips of their fingers touched, the letter held fast by them both. She stared up at him, her eyes a warm shade of green surrounded by brown lashes, pale skin and light red hair.

"I'm desperate, Jake."

With a sardonic lift of one eyebrow, he said, "Don't sugarcoat it on my account."

Her free hand covered her cheek, and she shook her head in exasperation. "I'm sorry. I don't seem to know what to say."

Jake shrugged away her apology. "It's an awkward situation. But you're right. We're both a little desperate. I need you in order to keep my land, and you need me so you can keep your daughter. This appears to be a match made in heaven.''

He wondered at the reason behind her slight gasp. When she tugged at the letter, he released it. The moment the contact broke between them, she flitted to the far side of the room, stopping at the bottom of the stairs. One hand on the railing, she said, "I saw you. At the cemetery. This afternoon."

From the corner of her eye, Josie saw Jake straighten his back and square his shoulders. She could feel his eyes on her, and she was trying to think of something to say, really she was. His mention that theirs would be a match made in heaven had already made her blurt out the last thing she'd intended to say.

Staring at the polished banister, she finally said, "I'm trying to imagine a houseful of boys shrieking and playing." She strolled away from him, running a hand along an intricately carved piece of oak trim running the length of the room. "You mentioned that your father died recently, your brother a long time ago. What about your mother?"

"What about her?"

The sharp edge in Jake's voice drew her around. He stood near a leather sofa, his shoulders squared, his expression severe, the shadow of a five-o'clock beard darkening his jaw and chin. There was an unusual glint in his eyes. She didn't intend to look deeper, but once she had, she couldn't look away.

"Did she die, too?" Josie asked quietly.

"No." He'd uttered the word succinctly, without a hint of feeling.

"Then where is she?"

"Last I knew, she was living in Texas with her newest husband."

"I'm sorry."

"Don't be. She left of her own free will when Cole and I were both kids. It doesn't matter."

Oh, yes it does, Josie thought. His mother had deserted him and his brother. What kind of woman could turn her back on her children? No matter what Jake said, it mattered a great deal. Intuition told her it wouldn't be wise to voice her feelings.

"Tell me about the men who work for you."

"You want to talk about my men?"

She paused at a shelf that she would have used to display family photographs and souvenirs from long-ago vacations. This shelf contained glass, bronze and pewter figurines of bucking broncos and longhorn cattle. It was probably an expensive collection, but it contained no whimsy, no warmth, no heart. Moving to the window, she could see the barns and sheds surrounded by painted fences. Farther away, the fences were weathered and gray, but still straight and well kept.

"The two men I saw yesterday weren't what I'd expected," she said. "A lot of the ranch hands I've met since moving out here are bandy-legged cowboys with a cheekful of chew and a tendency to yodel. Your men are different."

"The two you saw yesterday were Buck Matthews and Billy Schmidt. They both spend as much time in the Jeep as they do on their horses, so when they're bandy-legged, it's from sitting too long on a bar stool, not in a saddle. They're in their early twenties and are both saving to buy their own spreads someday. You're right about the cheekful of chew. They picked up the habit from Slappy Purvis, an old cowhand who's been with the McKennas since before I was born."

"Then there are three men working for you?"

"Technically there are four men on the payroll, but Sky

Buchanan considers himself a free spirit, not an employee.''

"A man named Sky?" she asked.

"When you meet him, you'll see it suits him. He drives too fast and sleeps too little, but he's the best roper in South Dakota, the best cowhand this ranch has ever seen. He's been here on and off since the summer we both turned seventeen."

Intrigued, Josie said, "Is he planning to buy his own spread one day, too.''

She sensed more than saw Jake shake his head. "Sky claims he has no use for land ownership. He also claims the only things he can't fix are a broken heart and the crack of dawn. He's working on the crack of dawn."

The deep undertones in Jake's voice drew her closer, until no more than three feet separated them. Jake McKenna was a hard man. It was what she'd expected. Steel and heat. His softness and humor surprised her, enticed her, into softening in return. Smiling up at him, she said, "Who does the cooking and the cleaning?"

"A woman from town comes out twice a week. The rest of the time I get by."

"Basically you're telling me that five tough single men work the second-largest spread in this part of South Dakota."

His eyes narrowed, and a muscle worked in one cheek. Just like that, the warmth and humor were gone, and the steely expression was back. Josie had never seen a faster change come over anybody. Although she didn't understand it, it didn't scare her.

She would have been worried if Jake had never known love, if his cold father and selfish mother were all he'd ever had. But Jake had loved his brother. And he respected his men and seemed to share a unique kinship with Sky Buchanan. Jake McKenna might have been gruff on the outside. Inside he had a heart. She was seldom wrong about these things.

"Did I pass?"

She stared at him, unmoving. When Josie was ten, she'd kicked a boy in the shins for sounding so condescending and sarcastic. Luckily she had more control over her temper these days. Besides, Jake McKenna might have had a legendary ornery streak, but underneath he was an honorable man.

"I suppose you could say you passed, although I hardly consider asking a few questions a test. If we're going to be sharing our lives for a time, I'll likely be asking more questions. Is there anything you'd like to ask me?"

Jake was at a loss for words, and he didn't take kindly to the sensation. Most women would have floundered beneath his glare. So would most men. Josie simply lifted her chin at a haughty angle and waited for his reply.

He thought about everything he knew about Josephine Callahan. She was a stubborn woman who was neither tall nor the least bit buxom. In other words, she was nothing like the kind of woman he'd assumed he would marry someday. His mind turned to the way she'd responded to his kiss a few nights ago. Questions? No, he didn't have any questions. He knew everything about Josephine Callahan he needed to know.

She glanced at her watch. "Oh, my. Kelsey will be out of school soon. She'll be afraid, if she gets home and I'm not there."

She breezed past him, straight out the door.

"Josephine, wait."

She paused, one hand on her open car door, her gaze climbing to his.

"We have several important matters to discuss."

"I know. I have to tell Kelsey. I'm sure she'll be tickled pink. And you'll probably want to have a prenuptial agreement drawn up. We have to set a date. I'll still have to close the store. I wonder how difficult it will be to sublet my apartment for a while. You're right. We have a lot to talk about. Could you stop over sometime after six? Mercy, I'm getting married again. I never thought I would. It's strange how things work out, isn't it?"

With that massive bit of understatement, she strode out the door, slid behind the wheel of her old sedan and drove away.

Jake watched until her car was nothing more than a speck on the horizon. He thought about heading back into the house, but made his way out to the barn, instead. Buck and Billy had taken the Jeep out to check on the herd grazing on the southern corner of the Lone M. Sky was working on machinery in the shed, and Slappy was checking fences along the eastern border of McKenna land. There was always work to do on a ranch, and nobody worked harder than Jake. Right now he needed to think, and the best way to do that was to saddle up King, his favorite horse, and ride until there was only man and horse and McKenna land as far as the eye could see.

Twenty minutes later Jake's mind had cleared and his future seemed secure. Halfway into the ride, he'd given King free rein, allowing the horse to set off at his own pace for his own destination. Jake wasn't surprised they ended up at Sugar Creek.

He dismounted, then led King down the bank for a cool drink. After slurping noisily, the big, black gelding nudged Jake aside and started to graze on the cool, moist grass growing on the creek bank. Resting on a fallen log, Jake watched the muddy water rush over rocks that had been worn smooth over the years. Later in the summer, the soil would be pitted from the hooves of the cattle that would come here to drink, and the grass would be little more than stubble.

Jake had never told anyone, but Sugar Creek was his favorite place on the entire ranch, possibly in the world. Cole had taught him to swim in a deep pool just around the bend. When he was ten and Cole was fourteen, they'd camped back here. They'd built a fire and fished with bamboo poles. Years later and a little farther downstream, Jake had kissed Emma Jane Parker and had tried to get past first base with her. Funny, the things he remembered. So many of his memories were centered here. Because of Josephine Callahan, this hundred acres would remain McKenna land.

Hoofbeats sounded in the distance, steadily growing closer. Within minutes, a familiar voice called down to Jake. "Slappy told me you rode off with a yowling yee-ha. I was sure he was mistaken, because I'm the one who whoops it up, not you."

Glancing up at Sky, Jake couldn't quite pull off an off-hand shrug.

"Oh, my God, Slappy was right."

Sky dismounted and joined Jake near the water. "What's going on, McKenna?"

Jake swept his right hand through the air. "Despite Isaac's stipulation, this land is going to remain mine."

"So Josie agreed to marry you, after all." Sky plucked a tall piece of grass and chewed on one end. "You ever think that maybe Isaac made that stipulation so his only surviving son wouldn't end up a snarling, lonely old man like him?"

Jake's *harrumph* came all the way from the soles of his boots.

"You're cheerful, McKenna."

"I try."

"Maybe you ought to try harder. Take some chances, loosen up a little, have some fun."

The two men watched the water flow past in silence. It was hard to know what Sky was thinking about, but Jake tried to remember how long it had been since he'd taken chances, loosened up, and had a little fun. It was easy for Sky. *Chance* was his middle name.

By unspoken agreement they both scaled the bank and mounted their horses. Riding toward the lane in silence, Jake knew Sky was itching to urge his horse into a gallop. A voice in Jake's head had him flicking the reins and nudging King with his heels. "Last one to the barn," he called over his shoulder, "has to muck out the stalls."

King surged forward. Behind them, Sky swore and urged his horse into the race. They sped toward the lane, the wind in their faces, their bodies curled low, strong legs gripping their steeds, pressing their mounts to go faster. By the time the barn came into sight, Sky was gaining on him. They sped through the open gate, Jake's mount a mere head ahead of Sky's.

Neither man said a word as they led the horses inside, the scent of oats and straw mingling with the pungent odor of dirt floor and horse sweat and old hay. Jake and Sky set about unfastening cinches and heaving their saddles onto racks. The minute they were finished, the horses headed for the fresh air in the corral, and Jake reached for a pitchfork.

Wrapping his fingers slightly above Jake's, Sky said, "You won the race."

"I cheated."

Sky winked. "Fun, wasn't it? Glad to see you have it in you. You're an engaged man with a wedding to plan. Go on. Get out of here."

Jake relinquished the pitchfork to Sky. He strode only as far as the door before turning around. "Sky?"

Skyler Buchanan took his time looping his hands over the tip of the pitchfork's handle and meeting Jake's gaze. "Yeah?"

"I'm going to need a best man."

Eyebrows raised, grin cocky, Sky said, "Ornery, you're a force to be reckoned with, McKenna...you smile now and then, and Josie Callahan isn't gonna know what hit her."

"Is that a yes?" Jake grumbled.

They shared a meaningful look, dust floating on slanted beams of light between them. With a slight nod, Sky trudged to the first stall. "That's a yes. Now if you don't mind, I've got work to do, and so do you."

Jake pulled into the alley and parked next to Josie's car. He hadn't spoken to her since she'd driven away from his place earlier that afternoon, but he took the fact that she'd turned the light on for him at the top of the stairs as a good sign.

Sky had been right. Jake had had a lot to do, a lot of plans to make. He didn't know what all had to be done from a woman's end, but he'd gotten started on the important things from his perspective that very afternoon. He'd arrived in Pierre just before the stores closed and had returned to the ranch with his purchase amidst a lot of bellyaching and swearing and hollering. Slappy Purvis had cut his hand on a rusty piece of machinery. The gnarly cowpoke lived in an old cabin in what could only be described as early squalor. He chewed tobacco and wrestled cattle for a living. He'd been known to stare down the orneriest bulls in the West, and yet it had taken three grown men to hold him down for the tetanus shot and eleven stitches Doc Kincaid had administered.

To top it all off, one of the horses had come hobbling in from the pasture. It took the local vet, Luke Carson half an hour to sew up the animal's front leg. It hadn't been a good day for flesh—man's or beast's. It was all in a day's work, but Jake had fallen behind. He'd planned to arrive at Josie's place in time to take her and her daughter out for a late supper. Now it was after nine. The diner closed at seven, and Kelsey was probably already in bed. Now that he thought about it, that wasn't necessarily a bad thing. What he had in mind might be better done in private.

He moved quickly, taking the steps two at a time. Josie must have been watching for him, because she appeared at the screen door when he was halfway up the stairs. His steps slowed as he studied her. She was wearing another of her dime-store dresses. It was orange and faded and harked back to the seventies. God, it was awful. It wouldn't have mattered if it had been a designer original. He still would have wanted to remove it, to stare long and hard at what was underneath, and to touch her and satisfy the burning need of a man for a woman.

First things first. He held Josie's gaze and slowly removed his hat. Drawing a small black box from his jacket pocket, he paused on the last step.

She opened the door and stood on the landing, he on the next step down. Their gazes were level. One tug and she would topple into his arms and he could kiss her, and all this thinking and reasoning, this burning desire to take her to bed would be over.

"Hello, Jake."

Was it his imagination or did she sound breathless? "Hello, Josephine."

Her gaze darted to his outstretched hand. Maybe the light was playing tricks with his vision, or maybe she'd always been pretty, and he'd been too blind to see.

"This is for you," he said very, very quietly.

Her fingers fluttered against the palm of his hand, conjuring up images that nearly buckled his knees. She opened the small box, and Jake had to remind himself to breathe.

"Oh, Jake, you shouldn't have."

He felt himself beginning to smile and his desire beginning to make its presence known.

"I can't accept it."

Jake swallowed hard, a cold knot forming in his stomach.

"It's too expensive. Goodness, Kelsey and I could live for a year on what this must have cost you. It's nice of you, but it's too much, Jake. Really."

Josie was staring at the diamond-and-emerald ring in the box in her hand, and failed to notice the chill that had grown between them. "I was expecting a prenuptial agreement, not a ring," she said matter-of-factly.

He scaled the top step and pulled her with him into her apartment. Glaring at her, he said, "Would you like to take out a full-page ad?"

Her face paled. Jake prayed to God it wasn't out of fear of him. He released her and paced to the far side of the room, tension stretching even tighter between them.

"Maybe you would prefer to put it on the six-o'clock news. Josephine Callahan and Jake McKenna Make a Marriage Deal. No Strings Attached. Wouldn't good old Charles and Gretchen have a field day with that?"

Her eyes grew round, her face deathly pale. She ran to the door and peered out. "Do you think they've hired private investigators. Did you see anybody unusual lurking in the shadows? What if somebody overheard? They'll use it against me. I know they will. They'll take Kelsey, and she'll grow up in that cold house like Tom did. They're older now, and wiser, and wouldn't let Kelsey escape the way Tom did."

Jake's anger dissolved by degrees. He told himself anger was all he had felt. Running a hand through his hair, he said, "You're marrying a McKenna. People will expect you to be wearing an expensive ring. And as far as private investigators go, I didn't see anyone suspicious when I pulled up. You're probably safe for now. But we have to make this look authentic. I've already asked Sky to be my best man. And I've spoken with Reverend Jones. He can see us tomorrow at two to make arrangements for the wedding."

"Reverend Jones? I thought we'd go to the justice of the peace."

He shook his head in a manner that left no room for argument. "This might be your second wedding, but it'll be my first."

She nodded slowly, her thoughts speeding ahead so quickly she failed to notice the grim set of his jaw. "If you want this to be a formal occasion, Kelsey will need something to wear. There's a second-hand store in Pierre. Maybe I can find her a dress there. I suppose I could get my wedding gown out of storage. It should still fit."

"No."

She turned her head to look at him. "But Jake."

"No seconds."

She felt on the verge of understanding something important about him. "Jake," she said with quiet dignity, "I don't have any money to buy another dress."

"Then I'll buy it."

"No."

It was his turn to look at her in surprise.

Meeting his stare, she said, "I won't take charity."

"It isn't charity, dammit."

"There's no need to swear."

"I said I'll buy you a damn dress."

"I heard you." She glanced over her shoulder. "Kelsey probably did, too. I'll think of something. When?"

His eyebrows drew down in consternation, *When what?* written all over his face.

She knew better than to smile, but she couldn't help sympathizing with him. It wasn't always easy to follow her line of thinking. "When were you, er, um, that is, how long do I have?"

Jake bit back a scathing retort and headed for the door, sputtering under his breath that she was getting married, not facing a firing squad. "Friday."

"Tomorrow?"

"No, a week from tomorrow."

She made a mental list of everything she had to do. Halfway through the list, she thought about the letter she'd received from Charles and Gretchen's attorney. The sooner she married again, the better. "A week from tomorrow sounds fine to me."

The banging of the screen door was his only reply. By the time Josie reached the door, Jake was halfway down the stairs.

"Jake?"

She knew he heard her because he stiffened, but he didn't pause until he'd reached the bottom. "Jake?" she called again, more softly than before.

His right foot was on the last step, his left leg bent at the knee. He turned and slowly looked up at her.

She opened the door. Striding as far as the edge of the landing, she extended her palm toward him, uncurled her fingers, and opened the box again. "The ring is lovely. Thank you very much."

He stared at her for a long time. Finally he said, "You're welcome, Josephine."

From this distance she couldn't see the expression in his brown eyes, but she could see the crease in one lean cheek. She wished he would smile. Yearning washed over her, reminding her of how lonely she'd been these past two years. Before she completely lost control of her senses, she said, "If we're getting married next Friday, we'll need to announce our engagement soon."

"Just wear the ring in public. The Jasper Gulch grapevine will take care of the rest. I'll pick you up tomorrow at a few minutes before two."

He placed his hat on his head, gave the brim a slight tug, then sauntered down the remaining stair. He looked up once when he reached his truck, but he didn't say anything, and neither did she. Watching until he pulled out of the alley, she thought his body language spoke volumes, but in a language she didn't understand.

She went back into her apartment, lost in thought. After going about the nightly rituals of picking up and straightening, she checked on Kelsey. She kissed her daughter's soft cheek, tucked the lightweight blanket under her little chin, then prepared herself for bed. Yawning, she crawled between the sheets in her tiny bedroom.

"Goodness gracious," she whispered to Tom. "In a little over a week, I'll be a married woman again. Jake is a good man. He doesn't laugh like you used to, but I think he'll be good to Kelsey and me. Because of him your parents won't be able to take our little girl, Tom. This really is the answer to our prayers, isn't it?"

She squeezed her eyes shut tight, listening.

"Tom?"

Her mind was fuzzy, and she couldn't seem to hear any reply. Turning onto her side, she yawned again. People always complained that they couldn't sleep when their lives were turning upside down. She was just the opposite. She'd always been a firm believer in two surefire cures. A hearty laugh and a long night's sleep. All alone in the dark, she didn't feel much like laughing, but she thought she could have slept until noon.

She couldn't, of course. Kelsey would be up by seven. After getting her little girl off to school, Josie would put a For Sale sign in the store's window. Sometime before Jake arrived tomorrow afternoon, she would have to remove the wedding ring Tom had given her more than six years ago and replace it with the diamond and emerald ring Jake had given her tonight. The idea sent a lump to her throat and tears to her eyes.

She thought about that letter and about Jake's father's will. She'd married once for love. She'd been lucky. In a sense she was lucky now, for although Jake didn't even pretend to love her, nor she him, their marriage would serve two very important purposes. For her sake and Kelsey's and Jake's, she would wear the ring in public. She would hold her head high. And she would pretend. And then she and Jake would meet with Reverend Jones to make arrangements for the wedding ceremony. She wasn't sure she could pretend in front of a man of God. Wasn't pretending the same as lying?

What choice did she have?

"I'm doing the right thing, aren't I, Tom?"

She listened, but the only sounds she could hear were the sighing of the wind and the rustle of the curtains at her window. Before long her eyes fluttered closed, and she fell into a deep, dreamless sleep.

Chapter Five

"It's true! I heard it, and now I've seen it with my own two eyes!"

Brandy Schafer tucked her pencil and order pad into her apron pocket and grasped Josie's hand. "Oh, what a gorgeous engagement ring! I'm just green with envy."

Josie smiled shyly. "Thank you," she murmured, discreetly trying to pull her hand out of the waitress's grasp. Brandy was five years younger than Josie and had a strong grip. She'd been one of the few girls in her graduating class to remain in Jasper Gulch. Pretty and outgoing, she'd earned good grades in school, but most of the time she let her quest for love get in the way of her common sense.

"It's so romantic. Isn't she the luckiest woman in the world?" she implored the other three women at Josie's table.

Jayne Stryker, Brittany Colter and Crystal Galloway all nodded. "Josie is very fortunate," Crystal agreed.

"I agree that she's fortunate, but I don't know that she's

the luckiest woman in the world," Brittany qualified. "I'm feeling pretty lucky these days, myself."

"But she's definitely lucky," Jayne said, eyeing the ring on Josie's hand from across the table.

Kelsey slurped her chocolate shake through her straw, drawing everyone's attention. Seizing the moment when Brandy's guard was down, Josie managed to wrestle her hand free, diamond-and-emerald ring and all.

"I wish I could find someone to love," Brandy whispered.

Crystal Galloway laughed, a deep, sultry sound befitting a woman with exotic green eyes and a body that had been known to stop traffic. "You're only twenty-one years old, Brandy. Your day is coming."

Rolling her eyes expressively, Brandy said, "You sound just like my mother."

Josie caught a flicker far back in Crystal's eyes. Was it pain? Sadness? There had been a lot of speculation concerning the reason Crystal had moved to Jasper Gulch a few years ago. Rumor had it she'd been something of a child prodigy. Some folks claimed that was the reason she was so good at keeping the men of Jasper Gulch at arm's length. Josie had a feeling there was more to it than that.

With a sardonic lift of one eyebrow, Jayne Stryker, the woman who had insisted upon coming to the diner to celebrate her latest business venture, watched the dramatic waitress saunter away. Every man in the place must have been doing the same, because one of them mumbled, "That gal sure knows how to advertise."

Old Cletus McCully snapped one suspender and shrugged. Others nodded, and somebody said, "These days the scenery here in the diner is as good as the food."

Jayne mumbled under her breath that some things never

changed. Brown eyes flashing, she said, "Now let me see this ring I've heard so much about."

Josie held out her hand for the twentieth time that day. Last night she'd been worried that she wouldn't be able to look people in the eye and pretend her engagement to Jake was real. As it turned out, she hadn't had to do a lot of pretending. She'd simply worn the ring to the grocery store a few hours ago. By noon, news of her engagement and upcoming wedding had been all over town. Now, at nearly one o'clock, several of the area bachelors were complaining that another single gal was off the market.

Speaking loudly enough for the men closest to her to hear, Jayne, the town's newest bride, said, "Don't you fellows fret. Josie's engagement to Jake is proof that the advertisement you Jasper Gents placed in the papers to lure women to this section of South Dakota worked."

"It worked for a while," Neil Anderson sputtered. "But the single women are almost all gone again."

"You leave that to me," Jayne said. "Josie has just sublet her store to me. The former five-and-dime is about to become headquarters for the mail-order catalog business I'm launching. Other new ventures will follow. By providing business opportunities and job prospects, we'll give the girls who grow up here a reason to stay, and new people will have a reason to move out here. It'll all work out, you boys just wait and see."

Most of the "boys" in the room were over thirty, and each and every one of them were tired of waiting for women to move to their fair town. They'd spent many a night across the street in the Crazy Horse Saloon, complaining to anybody who would listen about the string of long, lonely months they'd been forced to endure due to the shortage of women in the area. Lately, their rumblings had been carrying over to the diner and the barbershop and the feed store north of town.

"How long do you think these new ventures you mentioned will take?" Neil Anderson asked.

"Six months," Jayne replied.

"Six months!"

"A year at the most," she added wryly.

"Another whole year?"

"Aw, shoot."

"Dang."

"Blast it all, anyway."

Norbert, Neil's younger brother, eyed Josie's ring and shook his head. "Jake got the jump on us this time. Guess we don't have anybody to blame but ourselves."

"Maybe not," Neil agreed, meeting Josie's gaze. "But I was under the impression you weren't ready to date anybody, what with losing your husband and all."

Josie managed to cast a half smile at Neil before practically burying her face in the laminated menu. It wasn't that she had an interest in food. Even if she had, she knew the menu by heart. She didn't eat out often, but she helped the owner, Louetta Kincaid, in the kitchen now and then. Every night had its own special. Mesquite steak on Monday, meat loaf on Tuesday, rib eye and baby potatoes on Wednesday, scalloped potatoes with baked ham on alternating Thursdays, and three-siren chili on Friday.

Folks could get a cheeseburger, fried chicken or a sandwich any day of the week, and liver and onions the first Tuesday of the month. The place was more famous for its pies than its vegetables, but the main course, morning, noon and night was gossip. Josie was uncomfortable with gossip, especially when it centered on her. Really, she thought, staring at the words that had long since blurred before her eyes, she wished somebody would change the subject.

"Last we heard you weren't planning on getting married again," Forest Wilkie grumbled.

"Ever," Norbert added.

So much for Josie's wish coming true. She *had* told Forest she didn't plan to marry again. It had happened a few months ago when he'd invited her to dinner. She'd tried to let him down easy, explaining it wasn't him, but her. Now she wished she'd just said no.

"You and Jake haven't been seeing each other very long, have you?" Ned, the third Anderson brother quipped.

"So?" Brandy declared over her shoulder the moment she returned with her tray of desserts. Placing a slice of pie in front of Josie, she said, "Love isn't bound by time, Ned. Just look at what happened between Wes and Jayne."

Josie could have kissed the overly dramatic waitress.

"Brandy's right," Jayne said. "I never planned to marry again, either. I'd barely been here a week before Wes changed my mind along with my plans for the future."

Josie breathed a sigh of relief. Now that the conversation had shifted to someone else, she tucked the menu behind the salt and pepper shakers and reached for her fork.

"That is so-o-o romantic!" Brandy's hand fluttered to her heart. "Was it like that with you, too, Josie?"

Josie's fork clattered to the table just as the bell over the door jingled. Mertyl Gentry, an elderly woman who used to own the grocery store and now lived in the boarding-house with her gigantic cat, turned in her chair. "Tell us, dear. Did that dashing, brooding Jake McKenna sweep you off your feet the way Wesley swept Jayne off hers?"

Praying she wouldn't blush, Josie glanced around the table. Kelsey was looking at her with round brown eyes. Jayne, Brittany and Crystal were watching her, too, along with nearly everyone else in the room. They all wanted drama and details. A sense of inadequacy swept over her.

Doing everything in her power to depict an ease she didn't feel, she opened her mouth to answer, only to be interrupted by a deep baritone that sped up her heartbeat and thickened her throat.

"Are you ready, Josephine?"

She glanced up, straight into Jake's dark brown eyes. Ready? He was forty-five minutes early, and she hadn't touched her pie. She was overcome by a smile. "Yes," she said, placing her napkin on the table. "We're ready."

Jake was suddenly behind her, helping with her chair. Brandy looked as if she was about to swoon.

"Aw, shucks," one of the bachelors complained. "Now we'll never hear the details."

"I'll tell you this much," Jake said without taking his eyes off her. "Timing is everything. Isn't that right, Josephine?"

Josie was right in the middle of a nod when Kelsey piped up. "Jake! Me n' Mama are cel'brating on accounta I don't have school today and Mama subrented the store."

"That's good." Jake had spoken to Kelsey, but his gaze never left Josie's face. There was so much intensity in his expression Josie didn't even attempt to explain that the word Kelsey was looking for was sublet, not subrented. Warmth settled around her heart, the kind of warmth a person felt standing in a moonlit meadow when the sky was clear and the stars were bright, when everything in the world made sense.

Kelsey slid off her chair and took her mother's hand. And then, as if it was the most natural thing in the world, she tucked her other hand in Jake's big, work roughed one. The adults must have looked like giants from her vantage point. Kelsey grinned beguilingly, obviously in her element. Hand in hand in hand, the three of them started for the door.

"Now there," Brandy said behind them, "goes a man and a woman in love. Have you ever seen anything more romantic in your life?"

Glancing up at Jake, Josie felt herself easing into another smile. It was amazing. She'd been worried that it would be difficult to pretend that this engagement was real. Staring at the hard lines and contours of Jake's face, she didn't find it difficult at all, because the warmth sifting through her was real.

Kelsey skipped ahead to open the door, and Jake moved close to Josie's side. "Just keep walking, and keep smiling," he whispered.

Glancing over the tops of a dozen cowboy hats, she thought it was an odd request. Why wouldn't she keep smil—

Her gaze caught on a man she'd never seen before. She'd only been here a year and didn't know all the people in the area, but this man wasn't one of the local ranchers or cowboys. He might have been wearing jeans and a Stetson, but he had the stylish, useless look of one of those attorneys who advertised on television.

She didn't look at the man again, but she could feel his eyes on her. Heart racing, she gave Jake a smile she prayed looked more natural than it felt.

"Atta girl," he whispered close to her ear as she preceded him out the door.

Out on the sidewalk Josie had to remind herself to breathe.

"A friend of yours?" Jake asked, his eyes shaded from the midday sun by the brim of his cowboy hat.

He was staring at a relatively new, nondescript gray sedan parked along the curb. Feeling stricken, Josie said, "I've never seen him or his car before in my life. Have you?"

"There are just over five hundred people living in and around Jasper Gulch. I know every one of them. That man seated in the booth wasn't wearing a wedding ring, but he isn't one of the sixty bachelors who advertised for women a few years back, that's for sure."

Jake didn't believe in coincidences, and Josie knew Gretchen and Charles Callahan well. No matter what the man who drove this car did for a living, his little trip to Jasper Gulch had most certainly been funded by her former in-laws. They wouldn't do the dirty work themselves, so they'd sent someone to do it for them. The man was undoubtedly in Jasper Gulch to look for the dirt on Josie.

Her thoughts careened. Bit by bit Jake's sudden appearance in the diner made sense. He'd seen the car, and he'd come to her rescue. *Her* actions might have been natural, but Jake's had been orchestrated to serve a purpose. A very important purpose. She was immensely grateful. Why, then, was the warmth she'd felt earlier being slowly replaced by something so much colder?

She gave herself a mental shake. All Brandy's talk of romance must have gone to her head. Her upcoming marriage to Jake might have been an answer to her prayers, but it wouldn't last forever. She cared about him, and she was grateful to him. She respected him a great deal. But this was business. Okay, it was good business, but it wasn't love. It wasn't even infatuation.

Josie took Kelsey's hand as they crossed the street. Upon reaching his truck, Jake opened the passenger door. While her daughter scampered up, Josie said, "I think we fooled many of the fine folks of Jasper Gulch. We might have even fooled the stranger. Reverend Jones is next."

In lieu of a reply, Jake narrowed his eyes and closed her door with a brisk, firm click.

* * *

"Jake, my boy, it's good to see you," Reverend Jones said the moment he opened the door.

"Reverend," Jake answered. "This is Josephine Callah—"

"Yes, I can see that. Come in, come in. Excuse the mess. Smells good, though, doesn't it? Follow me."

Josie and Jake shared a look, then did as the good reverend instructed, the scent of homebaked cinnamon rolls heavy on the air. By the time they reached the office in the back of the parsonage, Reverend Jones was winded. Many pastors these days went by their first names—Pastor Bob or Pastor John. Once, Josie had asked Minerva, his wife of nearly thirty-eight years, why the man who worked so diligently to instill goodness in the hearts of his congregation went by Reverend Jones. Minerva had whispered, "He never felt Pastor Casper of Jasper Gulch would catch on."

Minerva Jones had an endearing sense of humor. Taking the seat he indicated on the other side of a marred old desk, Josie wasn't so sure about the reverend, himself. Recently he'd celebrated his sixty-third birthday. With his hardy paunch and sagging jowls, he looked older. She wondered how easy it would be to fool him.

"I understand the two of you wish to be married," he said, steepling his fingers beneath his double chin.

"Yes," Josie and Jake said in unison. "We do."

For some reason the preacher chose to stare long and hard into Josie's eyes, ignoring Jake. Clasping her hands in her lap, she wondered if he could see all the way into her soul. She hoped not, for although she knew that what she and Jake were doing was necessary, she dreaded trying to lie, especially to a man of God.

He turned his head and abruptly shifted his attention to Jake. "I've known you for a long time, son, although I've gotta say I'm still trying to find a way to get you to attend

Sunday services. Tell me, how does it feel to finally be in love?''

Josie very nearly gasped. Jake didn't so much as flinch. Gaze steady, voice even, he said, ''I wouldn't know.''

This time Josie really did gasp.

Reverend Jones's bushy eyebrows rose fractionally, his chair creaking as he leaned back. ''That's what I thought.''

Jake didn't fidget or stammer or bat an eye. Josie wanted to jump to her feet and demand to know what he thought he was doing. During the agonizingly long stretch of silence, he met her gaze. Suddenly she saw him with new clarity. Jake McKenna lived by a code of ethics that didn't include attending church on Sundays. He looked after his land and the people he cared about. He worked hard and expected others to, as well. He rarely smiled, and laughed even less. And he didn't lie, not to her, not to Reverend Jones, not to himself.

''I believe an explanation is in order, son.''

Running a finger along the brim of his black Stetson, Jake appeared to be considering his answer very carefully. Finally he said, ''Most people marry out of love. Last I heard, fifty percent of those marriages end in divorce. Josephine and I are marrying out of necessity. It's a private matter, but I can assure you that this union will be based on mutual respect and a genuine belief that we're doing the right thing.''

She'd been fiddling with the collar of her dress. Finding herself looking into Jake's eyes, she stilled her fingers. Beneath them, warmth sifted into the soft skin at base of her throat, slowly finding its way inside.

Reverend Jones released an airy whistle. ''While it's true that the divorce rate is high in this country, the divorce rate in this county is extremely low. Folks could argue that it's due to the shortage of women in the area. Although I prefer not to speculate too far outside my field of expertise, I happen to believe it's because folks out here are accustomed to hard work, and hard work is one thing marriage takes plenty of. Of course, the long, cold winters don't hurt, if you know what I mean.''

Josie felt her face turning pink and refused to look at Jake. Sex, er, um, sleeping together, that is, making love, or whatever one chose to call it, was one aspect of this arrangement they hadn't discussed.

The reverend began riffling through a stack of papers. Coming up with his day planner, he opened it, talking as he flipped through pages. "Ah, yes, a strong commitment is a good thing. Other than a little gold in his pocket and the widow he'd won in a poker game at his side, a strong commitment was all Jasper Carson had to offer his new wife. Legend paints Jasper as a rascal and Abigail as a righteous, proper woman who was spitting mad about the turn her life had taken. They married out of necessity and founded an entire town on the love that followed. It will be interesting to see what develops from your union.''

"What develops?'' Josie asked breathlessly.

The reverend nodded. "Abigail presented Jasper with three strapping sons. You and Jake are both young and healthy. Sometimes it's best to let nature take its course. Ah, yes, a strong commitment is a good thing, indeed. Now, did you want music and candlelight? Personally, my favorite part of a wedding is the buffet line. You are having a buffet supper, aren't you?''

"A buffet?'' Josie repeated, her gaze colliding with Jake's. This time he held up both hands and shrugged. "Of course,'' she said. "A buffet dinner and reception would be lovely.''

By the time they left the parsonage, they had not only chosen their music and two Bible verses to be read during the short ceremony, but they'd put together a guest list and had listened to the reverend's recitation of some of his favorite dishes they might want to include in the buffet supper that would follow, as well. Josie's heart beat an exaggerated rhythm all the while.

From the preacher's office they drove to the boarding-house where Kelsey was playing with Savannah Colter. Josie did her best to make small talk with Brittany, Savannah's mother. For some reason it wasn't easy. Within minutes she, Jake and Kelsey were on their way home. Josie told herself the reason she couldn't concentrate was that everything was happening so fast. It was no wonder her mind was reeling. So many plans had been made in so little time. The Ladies Aid Society had agreed to prepare the buffet supper, and the Anderson brothers were ready and waiting to play their boot-stomping country-western music at the reception. Surely the flutter of her heartbeat was a result of being caught in the whirlwind of wedding preparations.

In comparison Jake didn't appear flustered in the least. He drove with one hand on the steering wheel, one arm resting along the open window. He didn't mention Reverend Jones's reference to "letting nature take its course," but she noticed a smoldering heat in his eyes every time he looked at her. And he looked at her often.

It continued on that way for the next four days. She and Jake had gotten their blood tests and had applied for their marriage license. They'd issued invitations to nearly everyone they knew. Josie would make and decorate the cake, and Brittany had offered to organize the decorating of the town hall, while Melody Carson had insisted upon arranging flowers for the bouquets and centerpieces. Hearing that Josie's father had died when she was a child, Cletus McCully had graciously offered to walk her down the aisle.

Touched, Josie had kissed his lined cheek. The old softy had taken a white handkerchief from his back pocket and wiped his eyes.

She'd packed up some of her and Kelsey's things. She'd even helped Louetta out in the diner when Brandy had called in sick. She'd seen the stranger around from time to time and had heard through the grapevine that he claimed he was interested in settling in the area. Neither Jake nor Josie believed him, of course, but they kept their suspicions to themselves.

Josie felt breathless much of the time, while Jake, appearing calm and sure, continued to watch her, a simmering heat in his dark brown eyes. Bedroom eyes, Brandy Schafer had called them in a stage whisper when Jake had appeared a few minutes ago to pick Josie and Kelsey up from the bridal shower the Ladies Aid Society had held for her.

They loaded the lovely gifts she'd received into the back of Jake's truck. Arms filled a final time, the three of them walked down Main Street, Kelsey skipping ahead, Jake lagging behind as if he had all the time in the world to enjoy the warm May evening. Josie felt skittish and jumpy and was in no mood to *stroll* anywhere.

She knew what was at the root of her problem, and the heat in Jake's eyes wasn't helping. Like the wick on a stick of dynamite, it kept Josie stirred up and antsy. In three days she would be married again, and she would be sleeping in a strange bed, a wedding bed, and she wouldn't be sleeping alone. Part of the time she wouldn't be sleeping at all. She jerked so fast it was a wonder the package on the top of the stack in her arms didn't topple.

"Look, Mama," Kelsey called over her shoulder, pointing at the window display inside the town's only clothing store.

Relieved to have something else to think about, Josie

hurried to Kelsey's side. Staring at the items that had captured her little girl's attention, Josie's relief was short-lived. It was a girl's outfit, in Kelsey's favorite color, yellow. The shorts were denim, the shirt a soft knit in a matching shade. Blue-eyed puppies and green-eyed kittens with bows around their necks frolicked along the neckline and ruffled hem. It was a durable outfit with feminine appeal, right down to the matching yellow canvas shoes. It was way out of Josie's price range. Lately, gum balls were out of her price range.

"It's pretty, sweet pea," she said. "Let's go."

"But, Mama, I want it."

Josie heard the beginning strains of a whine in her child's voice. Firmly but gently she said, "The store's closed, Kelsey."

"Then let's come back tomorrow. Can we, Mama? Can we get it so I can wear it when you and me and Jake go to family day at school?"

"We'll see, sweet pea."

"We'll see means no." Chin touching her chest, Kelsey turned away from the display.

Tears formed in Josie's eyes, her gaze trailing to the small pair of white patent-leather shoes complete with an adorable little buckle and clicky heels nearby. They were the kind of shoes she would have loved when she was a child, the kind of shoes that would be perfect for Kelsey to wear to her mother's wedding in three days. The kind of shoes she couldn't afford.

Blinking her tears away, Josie looked up, only to find Jake looking at her little girl. He did a careful perusal of *her* next. There was something familiar about the expression in his eyes. Before she could place it, he reached into his pocket, and withdrew several large bills.

A sense of dread came over her, but she shook her head firmly, already following her daughter's trek to the truck.

"Take it." Jake's voice stopped her in her tracks.

She swung around, and suddenly she remembered where she'd seen the expression in Jake's eyes. Charles and Gretchen had looked at her the same way the first time she'd met them, and the last time she'd seen them, too, when they'd called her "white trash."

It was funny how the things that hurt the most wound up making a person strong. Leveling Jake a look she'd perfected on Charles and Gretchen, Josie said, "Put your money away, Jake. I don't want it."

He glanced all around. As if satisfied that no one was within hearing distance, he said, "Take it, anyway. Get Kelsey her play clothes so the other kids don't make fun of her, and get both of you something suitable to wear to the wedding. Preferably something that didn't come off a dime-store rack."

Josie's temper shot straight to the boiling point. Unwilling to give in to it in the middle of Main Street, she turned on her heel. Jake followed, his feet practically burning up the sidewalk between him and his truck.

Neither she nor Jake said a word during the ride to the alley behind the store. Kelsey sat between them, her disappointment forgotten, her little-girl sense of wonder and excitement over the upcoming family day at school all she could talk about.

"You are coming, aren't you, Jake?" she asked, her eyelashes batting as if straight out of a scene from *Gone With The Wind*. "Savannah says there are three-legged races and horsey rides, and the boys aren't s'posed to but they bring water pistols, anyway, and we get to chew gum and eat lunch outside."

Jake's and Josie's gazes met, held. She was the first to

look away. From the other side of the truck Jake said, "I'll see what I can do."

A moment later he pulled into the alley leading to Josie's apartment and cut his truck's engine. Josie got out, and Kelsey skipped around to Jake's side and immediately tugged on his hand. "Are you coming in, Jake? Are ya?"

"Oh, I'm coming in, all right."

His voice had been hard, the tone ominous. Josie had angered him. Tough. He'd angered her, too. What was wrong with the way she looked? Other than her daughter, Josie didn't have much except her pride. If Jake was ashamed of her, she wanted to know it before things went any further.

Unwilling to make a scene in front of Kelsey, Josie reached for a stack of gifts in the back of his truck, vowing to ask Jake point-blank as soon as Kelsey was asleep.

"Leave them."

She glanced up, straight into his eyes. Panic squeezed past her anger, choking it and her. Placing a steadying hand on the truck, she raised her chin a fraction of an inch and said, "What?"

"I said leave them."

She looked at the towels and cookware she'd received at the bridal shower. She'd known he was angry, but angry enough to have second thoughts about marrying someone like her? Swallowing convulsively, she said, "I know what you said. I'm trying to understand what's behind it. Are you telling me not to take the gifts inside because you've changed your mind about getting married and therefore we'll be returning them? Is that what you're trying to say, Jake? Is it?"

Chapter Six

A truck in need of a new muffler rumbled down the side street at the end of the alley. An old country-western tune filtered through an open window in the Crazy Horse Saloon next door. Birds chirped as they gathered in the trees for the night, and a sudden gust of wind whipped around the corner. In the midst of it all, Jake remained silent.

"Is that what you're saying?" Josie repeated. "Have you changed your mind? Because if you have, you're right. There's no sense carrying these gifts inside when I'll only be returning them, anyway."

Take it easy, the new voice of Jake's conscience whispered inside his head.

He was getting sick and darned tired of that stinking voice. Gritting his teeth, he glared at Josie. How in the world she'd gotten all of that out of "leave them" was beyond him. If he lived to be a hundred, he would never understand the way a woman's mind worked. It would take an eternity to understand Josie's.

"What the hell are you talking about?"

GET A FREE TEDDY BEAR...

You'll love this plush, cuddly Teddy Bear, an adorable accessory for your dressing table, bookcase or desk. Measuring 5 ½" tall, he's soft and brown and has a bright red ribbon around his neck – he's completely captivating! And he's yours _absolutely free_, when you accept this no-risk offer!

The Silhouette Reader Service™ — Here's how it works:

Accepting your 2 free books and gift places you under no obligation to buy anything. You may keep the books and gift and return the shipping statement marked "cancel." If you do not cancel, about a month later we'll send you 6 additional novels and bill you just $2.90 each in the U.S., or $3.25 each in Canada, plus 25¢ delivery per book and applicable taxes if any.* That's the complete price and — compared to the cover price of $3.50 in the U.S. and $3.99 in Canada — it's quite a bargain! You may cancel at any time, but if you choose to continue, every month we'll send you 6 more books, which you may either purchase at the discount price or return to us and cancel your subscription.

*Terms and prices subject to change without notice. Sales tax applicable in N.Y. Canadian residents will be charged applicable provincial taxes and GST.

If offer card is missing write to: Silhouette Reader Service, 3010 Walden Ave., P.O. Box 1867, Buffalo, NY 14240-1867

BUSINESS REPLY MAIL
FIRST-CLASS MAIL   PERMIT NO. 717   BUFFALO, NY

POSTAGE WILL BE PAID BY ADDRESSEE

SILHOUETTE READER SERVICE
3010 WALDEN AVE
PO BOX 1867
BUFFALO NY 14240-9952

NO POSTAGE
NECESSARY
IF MAILED
IN THE
UNITED STATES

Kelsey spun around, suddenly all ears. The little imp would have been curious at the sound of Jake's voice alone, even if he hadn't cussed. But cussing, my, that made things all the more interesting.

"Mama, is Jake mad?"

Josie was at a loss for something to do or say to defuse the situation. She was a firm believer in two surefire cures. A hearty laugh and a long night's sleep. Staring at the man glaring back at her, she couldn't have laughed if her life depended upon it. And sleep was still a long, long way off.

Jake's brown eyes appeared darker than she'd ever seen them. Where her anger had been red, his was black. She could tell by the black, layered look he gave her.

"Jake didn't mean to say a bad word, sweet pea. We're just talking. Run upstairs. We'll be right behind you."

"Promise?"

Josie's heart lurched at the sight of her little girl in her faded jeans and holey shoes, looking from one adult to the other. "I promise," Josie said.

"Do you promise, too, Jake?"

Jake turned his attention to Kelsey, his voice even and controlled. "Yes. We'll be up in a minute."

Satisfied that nothing was amiss, she grinned, revealing holes in her smile where two baby teeth had once been. Jake waited for the child to skip up the stairs and out of hearing range before shifting his attention back to Josie.

She stood at the back of his truck, her back ramrod straight, one hand clutching the tailgate. He knew how important this marriage was to her. Without it, she could lose her daughter. He was struck by her strength. She'd faced the world alone much of her life, at the mercy of fate and the powers that be. She was down on her luck and destitute, and it wasn't the first time.

Removing his hat, he ran a hand through his hair. He

allowed himself a calming breath and finally said, "If I had changed my mind about marrying you, you would have been the first to know. I merely meant that it would be unnecessary to carry all these gifts up to your apartment when we'll only have to carry them back down when you move to my place. Don't try to read between the lines, Josie. I say what I mean, and I mean what I say."

Without another word he turned on his heel and followed Kelsey up the stairs. His actions left Josie little choice but to do the same.

They spent the next hour pretending to smile, for Kelsey's sake. They both kept their inner turmoil carefully hidden. That, too, was for Kelsey's sake.

Completely unaware of the strong undercurrents in the air between the adults, Kelsey dropped off to sleep minutes after Josie tucked her in. Just like that, Josie was out of diversions. The time for pretending had come to an end.

She found Jake sitting in the chair exactly as he'd been before she and Kelsey had left the room. However, there was a new edge to his agitation, a kind of go-ahead-and-make-something-of-it jut of his chin. Following his gaze to the marred coffee table, she discovered what appeared to be two fifties and a hundred-dollar bill. "What are you doing, Jake?"

He took his time rising to his feet. "I want to know what's going on. Why you refused the money, when Kelsey obviously needs new clothes." He looked Josie up and down. "And so do you."

"I'm sorry if I'm an embarrassment," she said, attempting a casual pose.

"You're as sorry as I am nice."

She clutched the back of the wood rocking chair so tightly her knuckles turned white. "You're right. I'm not sorry. I'm not ashamed of how I look or what I wear. It's what's inside that counts. So don't do me any favors. Or is that the whole point?''

''Is *what* the whole point? What the hell are you talking about?''

''There's no need to swear. You've been watching me ever since Reverend Jones mentioned making love.''

''I've been watching you.''

''That's right. And stop repeating everything I say. You've been watching me, and I know you've been thinking that in a matter of days nature will take its course, just like Reverend Jones said. I won't tolerate your pity, Jake. And I won't accept your charity. Or was that money meant as a bribe?''

In the blink of an eye Jake was directly in front of her. He'd moved so fast she didn't have time to gasp, let alone retreat. She stared up at him, expecting an explosion. In its place was a deafening silence. A vein had popped out on his forehead, a muscle worked in his jaw and there was a distinct hardening around his eyes as he said, ''A bribe.''

He'd repeated what she'd just said, again. Josie thought better of reminding him of it. ''Perhaps you would prefer to refer to it as a trade,'' she said quietly.

His eyebrows rose, his only indication that he was waiting for her to continue. The problem was, she didn't know what to say. Her anger had deserted her, leaving her defenseless. How many times had her mama told her that temper of hers was going to be the death of her someday? Since it was impossible to undo something that had already been done, Josie took a deep breath for courage and said, ''We haven't discussed every aspect of our marriage. Certainly not the sleeping arrangements. I think I've always known, on an instinctive level at least, that a man like you wouldn't be satisfied with a marriage in name only. So you see, there's no need for any type of bribe or trade.''

Jake's blood rushed through his head with a roaring din. Out on the range, cowboys called a roped steer one that had been stretched. That pretty much described how he felt. Stretched, contorted, tied up in knots and unable to move. At least now he understood what had brought out Josie's anger. He'd injured her pride, and she'd retaliated. It was a natural reaction, one he understood well. Hell, he even admired her for it. And Jake McKenna didn't admire many people.

They hadn't bothered closing the screen door when they'd arrived. Over the top of Josie's head he could see the first moths of the season fluttering near the bare light-bulb. On a primal level Jake understood their need to charge the light, seeking heat despite the risk of getting singed. It was a risk every man in pursuit of a woman took. It occurred to him that that's what he was. In pursuit of Josie Callahan.

Hell and damnation, would wonders never cease?

As one second followed another, the knots inside him eased. Shifting away from her slightly, he spread his feet a comfortable distance apart and placed his hands on his hips, his gaze never leaving her face. "It's interesting that you used the word satisfied," he said, his voice deep and dark and quiet.

She stepped out from behind the rocker. Although she made no move to come any closer, she watched him closely. "It's true, isn't it?"

He shrugged. "It's true."

Neither of them moved. It seemed that neither of them could. Finally, Jake broke the silence. "I get the feeling that a woman like you wouldn't be satisfied with a marriage in name only, either. Am I right, Josephine?"

She probably knew her cheeks were pink, but she held his gaze, anyway, and damned if she didn't nod. He dropped his hands to his sides, when he would have preferred to put them all over her. "Just so we're both clear on the issue of sex."

Her blush darkened. Jake felt the strangest urge to grin. Since he didn't want to risk injuring something as fragile as her pride, he refrained, saying instead, "Then we both agree that sleeping together will be part of the marriage, not something we barter for or trade, certainly not something we do in payment of a bribe."

She nodded. "Agreed."

"Well, then," he said.

"Yes. Well, then." She quirked one eyebrow. When she smiled, so did he.

Josie didn't know what was happening to her, but she wouldn't have been surprised if she melted into a heap on the floor. Jake's smile did that to her. Maybe it was because it happened so rarely.

Maybe what she felt was relief.

Or maybe it was something else entirely.

As if reacting to a silent cue, they each took a backward step. Once she'd broken eye contact, she was able to stride to the coffee table, sweeping the money he'd left for her into her hand. Returning it to him, she said, "I appreciate your generosity, and I'll do my best not to embarrass you by wearing something old and faded to the wedding."

She could tell he wanted to argue and was deeply touched when he crammed his hat on his head instead and strode to the door. "It's branding time," he said over his shoulder. "I'm going to be out on the range with the men for the next two days, so I won't see you again until Friday. If you need to reach—"

"I can take it from here, Jake. I'll see you on Friday."

Josie thought he was going to smile again. His mouth looked all ready to, but then his gaze strayed to her neck,

to her breasts, to her waist and hips and legs. By the time
he made it back to her face, neither of them was up to
smiling.

"Friday," he repeated.

He gave his hat a slight tug. And then he was gone.

Josie didn't see Jake the following day, but she'd imagined him on his horse, rounding up cattle, roping bawling
calves, the sun hot on his back, the taste of dirt on his
parched lips, a course rope in his work-roughened hands.

She felt strange, thinking of another man. She told herself it was amazing that she had time to think, period. It
was Wednesday evening and she was packing up her
kitchen, and, as well, the wedding preparations were going
full speed ahead. Mertyl Gentry and Odelia Johnson had
stopped by that afternoon to confer with Josie about the
final details for the buffet supper they were in charge of
preparing. As soon as she'd picked Kelsey up from school,
they'd driven into Murdo, the county seat, to pick up the
marriage license. After supper Kelsey, so proud of her
fledgling ability to read, had produced a book and had pro-
ceeded to read aloud with so much gusto Josie had laughed
through the tears that had come out of nowhere.

Everything was going to be all right, she told herself.
And she meant it. Everything was going to work out just
fine.

After tucking Kelsey into bed, she stood at her open
closet, staring at her meager wardrobe. Everything else was
planned—the flowers, the cake, the music, the food. What
in the world was she going to wear?

The closest thing she had to anything remotely dressy
was a sundress she'd worn on her honeymoon with Tom.
Since Jake had balked at the notion of her wearing her
wedding gown, she doubted he would take kindly to her

wearing this. Besides, it was as faded and worn as everything else she owned.

She'd looked in a second-hand shop in Pierre and a consignment shop in Murdo. Neither place had anything within her price range that was appropriate for her to wear at her own wedding. It would have been a lot simpler if she'd swallowed her pride and accepted Jake's money. Simpler, maybe, but Josie had learned a long time ago that the simple way wasn't always the right way. She wasn't sorry she hadn't accepted his money, but she didn't have a solution, either. And the wedding was less than two days away.

Two days.

She tried to picture herself walking down the aisle on Cletus McCully's arm, Kelsey dropping daisy petals up ahead, Jake waiting at the front of the church, a hundred guests looking on as her eyes met his. Two images converged. In one she was wearing virginal white, and Tom was smiling at her from the front of church. In the other she wasn't wearing anything at all, and the man waiting for her had dark brown hair that touched his collar and dark brown eyes that glittered with appreciation and a masculine, seductive gleam.

Josie jumped at the sound of a knock on her door. Heart racing, she opened the door to the sound of Lisa McCully's sultry laughter. "I thought Brandy was exaggerating. I thought wrong."

"Lisa. Hello. Won't you come in?"

Lisa had been one of the first two women to answer the ad the Jasper Gents had placed in the papers a few years back. She'd opened the clothing store on Main Street and had married Wyatt McCully, who had been the sheriff back then and was now on a special task force with the police department in Pierre. Lisa was beautiful and dark, curvaceous and outgoing, the complete opposite of Josie.

Bustling into the room, she thrust a box wrapped in shiny silver paper into Josie's limp hands, then stepped back slightly. "Jake dragged me out of my house last night and asked—" Lisa's eyebrows shot up "—or should I say demanded, that I open the store for him. He managed to cool his heels while I finished nursing Rose, but man alive, I thought Wyatt was the epitome of still waters running deep. Jake isn't an easy man to say no to, is he?"

Josie smiled in spite of herself. "He doesn't particularly care for the word *no*."

Dark and sultry and more than a little brash, Lisa murmured, "Men rarely do. But they certainly make life interesting, don't they?" With a wink that had gotten her into plenty of trouble when she was younger, Lisa started for the door. "There. I promised Jake I would deliver the package and then leave you alone to open it. I'll see you on Friday."

Without another word, she left, leaving behind a befuddled Josie and a whiff of perfume.

Amid half-filled boxes in the middle of her kitchen, Josie stared at the package in her hand, wondering what Jake was up to. She carried the package into the next room. Gliding her finger beneath a length of clear tape, she removed the paper and lifted the lid.

Her lips parted around a silent "Oh." She didn't know what she'd expected, but it wasn't the pale yellow child's outfit nestled beneath a tuft of tissue paper. Taking out the outfit Kelsey had admired in the clothing store window, Josie discovered two pairs of shoes in the bottom of the box. One was yellow canvas, the other shiny white patent leather.

She hadn't said a word about those shoes. How could Jake have known?

Opening the small card, she began to read. "If you so

much as think of this as a bribe— Danged, stubborn woman. Until Friday." It was signed, simply, "Jake."

She sank into a chair, thinking, It takes one to know one. But she was smiling, just the same. Looking heavenward, she whispered, "You were right, Tom. Jake is a good man. But he's nothing like you. I'm not quite certain what a woman is supposed to do with a man like him. Tom? Are you there?"

She listened, but the only sound she heard was the wind in the trees and the beating of her own heart. She'd been so busy she hadn't talked to Tom in a while. Suddenly it seemed that he'd been gone from her for a long, long time. She tried to remember how his voice sounded and how he looked. Memories that had been so clear had become hazy around the edges, and made her sad.

She strolled about the apartment, lost in thought. She wondered if it was possible for angels to sulk. No, she didn't think so. Tom had never sulked. Jake was more prone to that. It was true that there weren't many similarities between Tom and Jake, but Tom had been a good man and so was Jake. Jake was also a proud man, and although she doubted he realized it, a kind one.

It seemed inconceivable to her that at least one of the girls who had grown up in Jasper Gulch hadn't seen past the sulk and moodiness to the heart of a decent man. It was a shame that nobody had loved him enough to stay, because Jake McKenna might have been a hard man, but he wouldn't have been hard to love. It wasn't fair that when he finally married, it would be in order to keep his land.

Josie sighed. She knew better than anybody that life wasn't fair. Just ask anyone who'd loved and lost, who'd suffered hardships or who had been born on the wrong continent or to people who didn't have it in them to care. Josie had known her share of sadness, but she'd also known incredible love. Her parents, her husband, her child. Jake hadn't been fortunate in any of those areas. It was no wonder the image he projected was all shoulders and sulk.

Her gaze strayed to the gift perched on the cluttered coffee table. There was more to Jake than broad shoulders and an aloof attitude. A lot more.

She strolled to the window overlooking the back alley. Pushing aside the curtain she'd found at a garage sale when she'd first moved to Jasper Gulch, the light caught on the diamond on her left hand. The ring was lovely, the emerald sparkling against the pale green fabric of the curtains. She hadn't asked for the ring or for the gift for Kelsey. And yet Jake had given her both. He was a man who gave more than he took. He deserved a proper wedding.

And a bride in a decent dress.

She eyed the curtains, a scene from *Gone with the Wind* creeping into her mind. A plan formed in her brain, and before she knew it, she was rushing into the kitchen for a chair. Suddenly giddy with excitement, Josie got busy.

It had worked for Scarlet O'Hara. Surely she could make it work for her.

Jake paced from one end of the pastor's study to the other. Running a hand across his bleary eyes, he turned when the door opened, cringing a little at the noise filtering through from inside the church. Skyler Buchanan put his hand to his own forehead as if he, too, had the mother of all headaches.

"Do you have the rings?" Jake scowled at the sound of his own voice booming inside his head.

Sky patted the pocket of his one and only suit. "Got 'em right here. You don't clean up too bad, McKenna."

Jake could have said the same thing about Sky, but it was better to keep as quiet as possible. They'd crammed four days worth of work into two days. Jake's back ached from too many hours in the saddle. His back wasn't all. He'd scrubbed his hands clean, leaving behind calluses worn raw from wielding a rope and a branding iron.

His mind was a little fuzzy, but he couldn't blame that on work. That he blamed on Sky, who'd insisted on throwing a party last night in Jake's honor. Billy had been three sheets to the wind in almost no time, Buck close behind. Slappy, who had forty years on them, hadn't passed out until well after two in the morning. In the end only Sky and Jake had been left standing, although their legs hadn't been fully operational, either.

It had taken Jake a considerable amount of concentration to get from the bunkhouse to the big house. Cursing his *former* best friend, Jake had fallen asleep fully clothed shortly after three. He'd awakened with a pounding headache at a little after six. Unfortunately a ranching operation didn't wait for its owner to get over a hangover.

Holding his head, he'd climbed out of bed. Bleary-eyed, he'd stood beneath the spray of the shower, the pummeling water helping to drown out the voice in his head that said, *I told you so.*

Ignoring his conscience, he'd downed a pot of strong coffee for breakfast, cursing Sky with every cup. They met up in the barn just about the time the sun was coming up. Going about their chores in silence, Jake's only consolation was the fact that Skyler Buchanan looked as bleary-eyed as he did. Served him right.

That had been hours ago. Jake wondered how many more hours it would take for his hangover to ease.

"Ohhh," Sky moaned, closing the door quietly. "Must have been that last drink."

Jake figured it was probably the last six.

"So you're really getting married," Sky said quietly,

pulling at the starched collar of his white shirt. "You're really doing what Isaac wanted."

Jake shrugged. "What choice do I have?"

"If Isaac is trying to make your life miserable, the joke's on him. I just saw Josie. What a way to go."

Suddenly alert, Jake eyed Sky more closely. "For a man with a hangover," he said, "you look awfully cheerful all of a sudden."

Sky grinned wickedly. "Oh, quit your scowling. Have I ever made you beg for details before? The woman's a vision, that's what she is. Her hair's piled on top of her head. Never have been able to figure out how women get it to do that. Maybe it's the hair and the heels, I don't know, but every bachelor out there is wishing he was in your shoes right now."

Organ music wafted through the door, the groom and his best man's cue to take their places at the front of the church. The two men started for the door, only to turn and face each other. Anyone else in a similar circumstance would have said something deep and meaningful. Jake and Sky shared a long look that made words unnecessary.

Sky went first, his stride as loose-jointed as cowboys of old. Jake followed more slowly. A dozen thoughts crossed his mind, among them a fervent wish that the organ had a volume control.

Josie waited at the back of church, surveying the guests sitting in the small church. She'd overslept that morning, and had felt a little behind all day. Strangely, she wasn't nervous. She'd certainly been flustered six years ago. She supposed there was something to be said for marrying for reasons other than love. She wasn't swooning, and butterflies weren't fluttering in her stomach. Instead she felt calm and serene.

It had been raining all day. The sky was still gray, but the clouds had lifted and the rain had finally stopped. The windows were open, the breeze carrying the scent of damp lilacs in full bloom, occasional gusts causing the flames on the tapered candles to flicker and dance. Brandy, who had been thrilled at the prospect of being Josie's bridesmaid, started up the aisle in the dress she'd worn for her senior prom. Josie had made hers and Kelsey's dresses from the same pale green fabric. Both dresses reached an inch or two below their knees, and both had been lovingly styled. The puff sleeves on Kelsey's dress had taken a half hour apiece to attach to the dress. Josie's was sleeveless, and simpler in design, the bodice formfitting, the neckline scooping in the front and in the back. She hoped she looked as regal as she felt.

"Okay, sweet pea," Josie whispered, placing a gentling hand in the middle of her little girl's narrow back. "I'll be right behind you."

Kelsey strode to the doorway in her shiny new shoes and promptly stopped in her tracks. For a second Josie thought she'd frozen in fear. But then the little sprite started down the aisle, and Josie realized that her darling daughter had simply been making an entrance.

"Ready?" Cletus McCully asked, his craggy face deeply lined, his brown eyes warm and as spry as Kelsey's.

Josie nodded. Together they started up the aisle, the daisy petals Kelsey had dropped fluttering slightly with their steps. Josie could feel all eyes on her. Since she didn't have half her daughter's aplomb, she kept her eyes straight ahead.

She'd fastened her wavy hair on top of her head and touched up the scuffs on her best pair of heels with ivory-colored paint. Everyone who'd seen her had said she looked beautiful. She knew better. Her hair was too red, her face too plain, her body too thin. Still, she thought she looked nice. In a matter of seconds she would know from the look in Jake's eyes if he was pleased with her efforts.

She saw him wink at Kelsey and could only imagine what Kelsey did in return. And then his eyes were on her. For a heartbeat time stood still.

She'd seen plenty of men in suits, but this was the first time she'd seen Jake in one. Her breath caught in her throat at the cut and fit. There was no Stetson on his head. Without it, his dark brown hair, shorter than it had been the last time she'd seen him, but still a little too long to be considered civilized, gleamed nearly black in the flicker of candlelight.

She was all set to smile, but Cletus brought her closer, and her eyes caught on Jake's face. The lines of his face were as strong as always, but his skin, bronzed by the wind and sun, looked a little—what? Pale? Green?

"Ready?" he asked, offering her his arm.

She nodded, whispering, "What happened to you?"

His reply was a small movement of his head, followed by a sharp wince. Josie glanced at Sky, who looked as green around the collar as Jake. Understanding dawned, and she smiled. All those hours of worrying that her best efforts wouldn't be good enough for a man like Jake McKenna had been unnecessary. She probably had Sky to thank for that.

His mission complete, Cletus backed away and ambled to the front pew. Placing her hand in the crook of Jake's arm, Josie took charge with quiet assurance. "That's it," she whispered, the soft green fabric of her skirt swishing as she led Jake the few remaining steps to the place Reverend Jones indicated. "This will be over soon."

"Dearly beloved, we are gathered here today..."

She stood in the front of church, Jake on one side, Kelsey

on the other, a hundred and some guests looking on. She wished...

What? That at least one of those guests was a special friend of hers? A long-lost relative? As far as Josie knew, she had no living relatives. But Kelsey was here, and she was the most important person in Josie's life. As the reverend's words flowed around her, she gathered strength, along with the conviction that everything was going to be all right.

Although she tried to concentrate on the low drone of Reverend Jones's voice, her mind wandered to the near future. The words didn't matter. They were just a formality anyway. In a matter of minutes she and Jake would be married, and Charles and Gretchen would have no grounds on which to base a custody suit.

"If anyone can show just cause why this marriage should not take place," Reverend Jones said in the same monotone voice he might have used to ask if they were having beans for supper, "speak now or forever hold your peace."

Without taking so much as a breath, he turned to Jake and Josie and said, "Now if you'll face each other and join your right hands."

"Not so fast, Reverend." A voice rang out over the quiet congregation.

From his position on the step where he always performed the ceremony, Reverend Jones glanced over the tops of Jake's and Josie's heads. "I beg your pardon, sir?" he asked.

"I said not so fast."

A murmur went through the church. Pews creaked and folks whispered behind their hands. Josie and Jake turned around just as the man they'd seen in the diner strode up the aisle.

"This wedding is a sham. A hoax."

"Who the hell are you?" It was Jake's voice, deep and hostile and loud enough to rattle his sensitive head.

The man had the gall to smile. "My name is Theodore Madison Abernathy III. I'm an attorney, and I have it from a reputable source that this marriage is a sham. The wealthy landowner and the, well, suffice it to say that this marriage will serve poor little Josie Callahan well."

A gasp went through the crowd. Jake's fingers curled into fists at his side. Only Reverend Jones remained calm. "Do you have proof, Mr. Abercrombie, was it?"

"Abernathy."

The reverend waved a hand through the air. "Whatever. Do you have proof that either Jake or Josie is not free to marry? If so, let's hear it. Otherwise, take a seat."

Theodore Madison What's-His-Name made a show of looking at the guests all around him. The man was tall, tanned and athletic, and appeared to be accustomed to the finer things in life. Hands on his hips, he might as well have been surveying a jury. He was decked out in natural fibers, from his designer suit, his silk tie, Italian shoes and hand-tooled leather belt. Only his smile was fake.

"I assure you that this marriage is a farce," he said in a voice he'd honed on rich clients. "How long have McKenna and the Callahan girl known each other?"

"Why," Isabell Masey exclaimed with so much vehemence her pointy little chin wobbled with indignation. "I never!"

"And neither will they. I have reference books that display a stronger attraction for each other than these two do. Have any of you even seen them so much as kiss?"

The church, all at once, was utterly quiet. Josie's blood seemed to slow to a crawl and then stop, right along with her heart. She glanced at Kelsey, who looked bewildered and ready to cry. Josie felt sick and, worse, helpless.

A large, callused hand encircled her arm, slowly drawing her around. Her gaze climbed to Jake's just as a tear trailed down her cheek. His hand glided to her shoulder, to her neck, to the side of her face. Through the roaring din in her ears, she heard him say, "This is a little like putting the cart before the horse, but relax, Josephine. And kiss me."

Her breath caught in her throat, and her eyes widened, only to flutter closed as his face lowered to hers.

Chapter Seven

Relax, Josephine, and kiss me. Kiss me. Kiss me.

The phrase stuck in Josie's head like a needle on a scratched record. Jake wanted her to kiss him, in front of Reverend Jones and the guests and Theodore Madison What's-His-Name.

Kelsey pressed her little body against Josie's side. "Who's that man, Mama?" she whispered. Her eyes were huge. "Make him go away."

Placing a gentle hand on the side of her daughter's face, Josie smiled weakly. She glanced up at Jake next. Gathering her wits, she went up on tiptoe, prepared to do her share to ensure that the brush of lips and air would look convincing to the man who would undoubtedly report back to Charles and Gretchen Callahan.

With a strong sense of purpose, she tilted her head slightly, her hand finding its way to the lapel of Jake's jacket as his palm glided to the small of her back. Their lips met, lingered, parted. The breath rushed out of her as her desire rushed in. Where she'd expected air, there was heat; where she'd expected the mere brush of lips, there was intimacy and urgency.

The kiss went on, enhanced by her gentle sway toward him, the warmth in his hand, the heady sensation of his mouth moving hungrily against hers. Her thoughts spun, her emotions whirled and skidded, a shock of pleasure running through her body. Jake's heart rate soared beneath her hand, his muscles corded as if he was fighting the need to drag her even closer.

A sound, repetitious and annoying, filtered through her haze of passion. It came again. And again. The clap of a single pair of hands echoing through the church. Jake eased back. Now that Josie could breathe, she could also think, but she couldn't speak.

The uninvited guest had no such problem. "Well done. It barely looked fake. You two ought to be in pictures."

Jake turned his head so slowly every man in the place took a collective breath. A blush had crept to Josie's cheeks, and there was a dazed expression in her eyes. His head was strangely clear. It seemed he'd discovered a cure for the common hangover. He shot Theodore Madison What's-His-Name a quelling glare. "I'm a rancher. A damn good one, but I'm not an actor."

"Damn right," Buck Matthews said, wincing as he jumped to his feet. "Pardon my French, Reverend."

"You aren't welcome here, mister," one of the other area ranchers called from a couple of rows back.

"So either put a lid on it..."

"...or leave."

The outsider eyed Jake's hired men, and then the other people who were looking at him with venom in their stares. It was highly likely that the man was completely lacking in scruples and honor, but he wasn't stupid. Smoothing a hand down his expensive jacket, he fastened the top button, looked down his nose one last time and left without another word.

A buzz started through the crowd before the door had slammed.

"Yep," Cletus McCully said to his granddaughter, Melody Carson, "things sure have been interestin' around here since the local boys put that ad in the papers luring single gals to our fair town. Mighty interesting indeed."

Josie's thoughts spun all over again, everything inside her swirling together in a slow, dreamy spiral. She'd been so calm before, so collected and in charge. Suddenly the faces of people she'd seen nearly everyday for a year swam before her eyes.

Josie?

She was warm, despite the light fabric of her dress and the breeze wafting through the church, and her blood was chugging through her head, making her feel tipsy, and she'd never been drunk in her life. She didn't know what was happening to her, but she couldn't think. She could hardly hear.

Josie?

She turned her head slowly.

Psst. Josie.

Was somebody calling her name?

Everyone was looking at her, but it was her bridesmaid who was moving her head repeatedly in insistent little gestures.

"Do you, Josephine?" Reverend Jones asked.

"Do ya, Mama?"

For a moment Josie couldn't fathom the question. Did she what?

"Do you take this man to be your lawfully wedded husband?" the preacher said again.

She glanced up at Jake. His eyes reflected the glimmer

of candlelight and sent her a private message. She must have answered Reverend Jones's question, because when she finally came out of her daze, Kelsey was holding Brandy's hand, and Jake was kissing her again, this time as her husband. Her knees went weak, and her thoughts spun all over again.

They started down the aisle. Behind them Kelsey giggled with glee, and a hundred and some tongues began to wag.

"Nice weddin', Jake."

"That's right. Real nice."

"Leave it to you to go out with a bang!"

"The nerve of those...those people! Trying to take Josie's little girl and sending someone to spoil your wedding."

"Some people are rotten to the core."

Jake nodded in the general direction of the local boys who had gathered around him at the punch table, but he kept his new wife in his line of vision. He and Josie had made the rounds together, greeting guests, thanking everyone for coming, dodging pointed questions. Jake was a pro at dodging pointed questions.

It was raining again. The sky had been so gray night had fallen without anyone's notice. The Anderson brothers were tuning their instruments in the corner, and Reverend Jones was taking a final trip through the buffet line. Jake wondered how much longer he had to wait before he and Josie could leave.

She was talking to several members of the Ladies Aid Society on the other side of the old town hall, probably thanking them profusely for the meal they'd prepared. The overhead lights threaded her pale red hair with gold. Several strands had fallen around her neck and ears, but the majority remained a swirl of waves on top of her head.

Maybe it was the hair or the heels or the fit of that pale green dress that put Jake in mind of a willow switch swaying in the wind, tall and fragile and winsome. Lovely.

"Folks'll be talking about this for years."

"'Yep,' they'll say, 'That Jake McKenna sure handled that city fella.'"

"Ain't that right, Jake?"

"Jake?"

"Where's he going?"

Moments before Jake strode out of hearing range, he heard one of the boys say, "Probably gonna go save Josie from the clucking tongues of the Ladies Aid Society."

That, Jake thought as he made his way toward Josie, wasn't what he had in mind.

"Look," Brandy Schafer exclaimed as he neared. "I do believe Jake has come to ask his wife to dance."

Dancing, Jake thought, meeting Josie's gaze, wasn't what he had in mind, either. With a quirk of one eyebrow, he studied the woman he had just married. Her cheeks were flushed, her eyes soft and dewy, a small smile on her lips.

"I haven't danced in a long time," she said quietly.

He supposed one slow dance wouldn't hurt.

While Brandy sighed dramatically behind them, Jake led Josie onto the small dance floor and turned her into his arms. "Hmm," she whispered, falling into step. "I didn't know you liked to dance."

"It was Billy's and Buck's idea. They thought I should save you from the town gossips."

Josie shook her head slightly before settling it close to Jake's chin. "Next thing you know the kettle will phone the pot to tell her she's black."

The surprising rumble of Jake's chuckle wrapped around her like strong arms and a secret smile. If Josie had been looking, she would have noticed all the heads that turned in their direction at the strange and unfamiliar phenomenon of a McKenna laughing. Instinctively she closed her eyes and simply enjoyed the dance. After all, it was her instincts that had brought her to this point in her life. She saw no reason not to trust them further.

Despite Charles and Gretchen's efforts, the wedding had gone extremely well. Kelsey had gone home with Clayt and Melody Carson, who had insisted that it wasn't exotic locations that honeymoons needed, but privacy. Tonight at least, she and Jake would be alone.

Jake drew Josie closer, the strum of guitar, the thrum of base and the low roll of drums nothing compared to the crooning melody and throbbing rhythm spreading through him. Luckily the steps were simple and required no concentration, because his mind wasn't on the music. That kiss had been burning in his memory, the effects burning in the very center of him for the better part of three hours.

Josie's body fit his so perfectly, he wanted to roll her underneath him and finish what that kiss in church had started.

He bent one knee and rotated his hips. It was no use. A need had been building in him all day, all week. And there was only one way to satisfy it.

His steps came to a stop in the middle of the song. "It's time we were going."

She drew away far enough to look up into his eyes. "Yes."

That was it. A simple yes, and a glimmer deep in her green eyes letting him know that a need had been building in her, as well. There would be no second places tonight. Tonight would be a first, for both of them.

The heels of Josie's shoes clicked on the polished wood floor as she preceded Jake through the door he held for her.

She noticed the nice touches instantly, the lamp turned low in the next room, the bowl of fresh fruit on the spotless kitchen counter, the bouquet of spring flowers in the middle of the oak table.

"It looks as if Muriel has been here again today," she said, slipping out of her rain-soaked shoes. Josie had met Muriel Olson yesterday when she and Kelsey, with the help of Jayne and Wes Stryker, had moved the rest of their things out to the ranch. Muriel was gray-haired and large-boned. She'd been up to her wrists in bread dough and had introduced herself without bothering with a handshake, declaring that it was about time Jake was getting married. Boasting a bossy disposition and a penchant for gossip, she hadn't even tried to cover her disappointment when the details she'd been hoping for hadn't been forthcoming.

"The house is lovely, Jake."

Warmer, she wanted to say. Almost inviting.

She met Jake's gaze and went momentarily still. The invitation wasn't in the flowers and fruit. It was in his eyes.

She swallowed, unsure how to take the next step. They'd talked during the ride from town, about inconsequential things mostly, like how disappointed Brandy had been when she didn't catch the bouquet and how mortified Crystal Galloway had been when she did. Now that Josie thought about it, she'd done most of the talking.

"Well," she said. And since her hands had a tendency to flutter, she clasped them in front of her. "I could put on a pot of coffee."

Moving with purpose, not haste, he started toward her. He held her gaze, loosened his tie. She wished he would say something. Do something. To put her at ease.

Jake was aware of the nervous flutter in Josie's eyelashes. If he'd been more of a conversationalist, he would have told her how lovely she looked standing in his kitchen, how pretty her hair was, styled that way, how deep her eyes appeared and how lithe and winsome and graceful she'd felt in his arms during that brief slow dance.

He reached for her hands, laced so tightly together. "I really don't want coffee." Unclasping her fingers, one by one, he whispered, "Do you?"

She shook her head ever so slowly. Something shifted in Jake's chest. He swore a corner of his heart had cracked open. He knew women liked flowery praises and honest compliments. He wanted to offer a few to Josie, but suddenly there were no words. So instead he kissed her. When she sighed, he swung her into his arms and carried her to his room. It wasn't difficult. She was a featherweight, soft as only a woman could be, and warm and agile as she shifted in his arms and slowly glided down his body until her feet touched the floor.

Josie felt her eyelashes flutter down, her breathing deepen, her body instinctively shift closer. In the light of day, Jake was a man of few words. In the dark of night, he didn't speak at all. Other sounds swirled around her. Her zipper rasped as he lowered it; his breathing rasped, too. There were sighs and kisses, and her dress gliding from her shoulders, landing on the floor with a quiet swish.

She could see the golden glow of the lamp through her closed eyelids. There were other sensations, too. Jake's coarse hands on her shoulders, whisking away her slip and underclothes. One of his shirt buttons pinged in his haste, a belt buckled clinked, shoes thudded to the floor. She heard as well as felt his hands find her again, covering her breasts. More sounds and sensations followed, her cry of pleasure, and his, the creaking of the bed as it accepted their weight, her moan as she accepted Jake's.

In the place of words, there were rampaging heartbeats and hitched breaths and long, drawn-out sighs. Josie's hands roamed, glided, seeking pleasure and reveling in it. Sweat glistened on Jake's back. His muscles were corded in places, rippled in others, his body lean and strong and degrees warmer than her own flesh. It had been so long. How could she not have known how much she needed, wanted, desired?

He kissed her, over and over and over, and when he wasn't kissing her, he was learning her, and she him, until she thought she was going to have to do a little bossing of her own. With one last kiss, he rolled her underneath him. Her eyes opened, and she watched the expression on his face, so intense, so in tune, so enthralled as he made them one. Together their bodies shifted, settled, surged—giving, accepting, taking, demanding. It was music, a dance as old as time. He never spoke, and neither did she. Where they went, words weren't necessary.

They surfaced slowly, the breeze wafting in the open window cool on their dampened skin. Josie sighed and all but purred, the instant he pulled the quilt around them.

Jake leaned back against his pillow, only to release a little groan. Fishing a hair clasp out from underneath his back, he rolled to his side. "Josie?"

Silence.

He went up on one elbow. Sidling closer, he slid his hand over her hip. She sighed again, and Jake looked closer. Her eyes were closed, her eyelashes a dark shadow on her cheeks. Her hair was a mass of waves and tangles, her shoulder bare.

"Josie?"

She didn't so much as bat an eyelash. The woman was amazing, intriguing and sound asleep.

Lacing his fingers beneath his head, he stared at the ceiling, redefining what made a woman sensual. In the past he'd thought it was tight clothes and plenty of cleavage.

Josie had neither of those things, and she'd practically knocked his socks off, if he'd been wearing socks, if he'd been wearing anything other than the grin that seemed to have taken up residence on his face.

Of course she was sleeping. She was tired, exhausted really, and no wonder. She'd closed her store, packed up her apartment, moved and put together an entire wedding in seven days. A yawn overtook him, reminding him of all the hours he'd spent in a saddle out on the range, and then at the impromptu bachelor party Sky had thrown for him last night.

Relaxed, sated, and the closest he'd been to happy in a long, long time, he closed his eyes and drifted off to sleep.

It was pitch-black outside when he opened his eyes. The room was dark, too. Josie must have turned off the lamp.

Josie.

A powerful jolt ran through him, bringing with it a shock of desire. It was a damn pleasant shock, made stronger by the memory of how Josie had felt in his arms and by the knowledge that she was only an arm's length away. He rolled over, already reaching for her. His hand came into contact with the quilt and the mattress and thin air.

Going up on one elbow, he switched on the lamp. Sure enough, Josie's side of the bed was empty. He wondered where she was. Had she awakened hungry and was right this second snacking in the kitchen? He wondered how she would react if he crept up on her from behind, if he drew her against him, and slid his hands in opposite directions along the front of her. He would turn her in his arms eventually, but not before a sigh escaped her lips and her head lolled back to rest below his chin.

His feet hit the floor before he'd made a conscious decision. Never one to roam his house buck naked, he pulled on his dress pants. Raising the zipper, he left the button unfastened and followed the faint glow of lamplight into the hall, the memory of how her soft flesh had felt in his hands making his steps light, his stride long.

He caught a glimpse of her in the living room. At the sound of a sniffle and a muffled whimper, the uncharacteristic grin slid away, his hands falling limply to his sides. Holding very still, he stayed in the shadows just outside the doorway.

Josie was sitting in his father's old wing chair. Her hair was down, the lamp turned to its lowest setting, her eyes closed tight as she rocked back and forth. Her cheeks were wet. In her hands she held a picture frame. And on her quivering lips was her husband's—her first husband's—name.

Jake's head pounded. His breathing all but ceased. The tiny opening in his heart ached for a moment, and then, as if someone had cemented the fissure, it closed up harder and tighter than ever.

He turned, and as silently as he'd left his bed he returned to it. Alone.

Josie always dropped off to sleep in an instant, only to awake one layer at a time. She wasn't grouchy in the morning, but she didn't feel human until after she'd had her first cup of coffee. Feeling languid, her body strangely tender, she breathed deeply and rolled to her back. Something was different.

She cast a groggy eye at the clock. And bolted upright. Oh my gosh. It was eight-thirty. Where was Kelsey?

Her memories washed over her in one huge wave, bringing everything into startling focus. The wedding, the reception, Kelsey waving goodbye as she left with Melody and Clayt Carson. Making love with Jake.

She wasn't certain what had roused her in the night, but she'd wakened shortly after two. The lamp had been on, Jake's arms around her. A blush had crept to her face at the memory of what she'd done, how she'd reacted. She'd been married for five years, had been very happy and content with her young husband. And yet she'd never reacted like *that*, had never been so aggressive, so wanton and greedy, as if she might just fly right apart in his arms.

She'd slipped out of Jake's bed and, wrapped in her comfortable bathrobe, she'd padded to the dresser where she'd placed Tom's picture days earlier. Enfolding it in her hands, she'd strolled out to the living room and had told Tom about the wedding and Kelsey's new shoes and the curtains she'd made into dresses for them. She'd listened with all her might, but she hadn't been able to hear him, and she couldn't remember how his voice had sounded.

And she'd cried.

The cry had been good for her, another stage of her grief. When she'd finished, she'd dried her cheeks and run her finger along Tom's face in the picture. She'd mourned him for two years. She loved him still. A part of her always would. But he was gone, and she was alive, and she was going on.

Leaving Tom's picture behind, she'd crawled into bed with her new husband. Snuggling close, she'd fallen asleep to the sound of Jake's even breathing and the feel of his heart beating beneath her hand.

Now it was morning, and she was all alone, smack-dab in the middle of his king-size bed.

She wondered where Jake was. Out on the range, probably. Too bad, she thought, her body warming, her thoughts whirling. She hadn't even had breakfast, yet she wanted to do that again. She was twenty-six years old. Maybe she was in her prime. A grin, wicked and womanly slid across her face. More than likely Jake was, too.

She crawled out of bed, slipped into her robe and strode out to the kitchen. Helping herself to a cup of coffee Jake must have brewed hours earlier, she wondered what he liked for breakfast and realized there were a lot of things she didn't know about the man she'd married. One thing she did know, though, was what he liked in bed. Another sultry grin spread across her face. Considering that they hadn't known each other very long, she figured she knew a great deal. The rest was just going to have to wait until Jake returned.

The sound of hoofbeats drew Josie around to the side of the house. Shading her eyes with one hand, she watched as man and horse galloped toward the barn. The horse was big and black. The man was Jake.

Anticipation had her smiling long before he emerged from the barn. "Good morning," she called. Feeling light-hearted, buoyant almost, she spread her arms wide. "Wouldn't this spot make a beautiful flower garden? With it's southern exposure and evening shade, I could grow almost anything."

Jake stopped several yards away. His feet were planted, his stance wide, his hips thrust foreword slightly, his Stetson low on his forehead. He was a sight to behold. Why wasn't he coming closer?

"Do you know why I think so many women like ranchers and cowboys?" she asked.

The critical glint in his eyes made her wary. She continued, but with more caution. "It's because they look disreputable, maybe even a little dangerous. Is something wrong?"

Jake felt a tightening in his throat and chest. Damn right

there was something wrong. He'd caught his wife crying over another man hours after *he'd* made love to her. And now she was standing in a patch of morning sunshine, looking radiant in her dime-store dress, and he wanted to make love to her all over again.

"Jake?"

"Don't you have anything to wear that isn't faded and at least ten years old?"

The smile slid completely off her face. She glanced down at her dress and then back at him. He felt like an ogre. Worse, he felt like a damn monster. Angry at her for being in love with a dead man and at himself for reacting to the sight of her in the same dress he was protesting, he forced his voice into a tone that was both calculated and exact. "Now that you're married to me, you can afford to buy decent clothes."

It was the word *decent* that brought Josie's head up and her shoulders back. If he'd said *new* or *pretty* or even *suitable* she might not have felt quite so cold. But the way he'd said *decent* implied that she was inferior, and she really resented that kind of snootiness.

"I don't know what kind of burr you have up your—" she paused for effect "—nose, but we've already covered this particular topic. I like the clothes I have. But I don't like people looking down their noses at me. I had my fill of that from Charles and Gretchen. I have to say you're not bad at it, but it would take you a million years to do it with as much blue-blooded hypocrisy as they did."

Jake had to hand it to her. She didn't stay down long. And when she came up, she came up swinging. For a moment he was sorry he'd hurt her. But then the image of her rocking back and forth, clutching *Tom's* picture to her breast rammed into his mind, and instead of apologizing he kept his distance.

"If your first—" he practically choked on the word "—husband's parents have so much money and social status, why haven't they at least taken care of their son's expenses?"

Her voice, when it came, was several decibels softer and much more subdued. "It's their way of punishing me for marrying their son. You see, they had big plans for Tom, and those plans didn't include marrying a girl like me. Thank God Tom was nothing like them."

A shudder passed through Jake, stirring up emotions, squeezing off his air. He recognized the sense of inadequacy and the inevitable realization that he would always stand in the shadow of those who had come before him. First Cole and now Tom.

He removed his hat, fidgeted with it for a few seconds. "They should have thanked you."

Josie did a double take.

He took a step toward her, stopped. "Tom's parents. Good old Charles and Gretchen should have thanked you. Because Thomas Callahan was a lucky man."

Josie stared at him, baffled and, darn it all, touched. She lifted a hand toward him, but he'd already turned. Cramming his hat on his head, he strode toward the house.

She was left standing in a patch of morning sunshine, staring after the man she had married but didn't come close to understanding. Last night he'd been ardent and passionate. This morning he was distant, and yet he'd paid her the highest compliment she'd ever received. Some people might have balked at the notion that a man who had suffered so much pain the last few days of his life only to die shortly before his twenty-sixth birthday had ever been lucky. But Jake hadn't been talking about Tom's pain. He'd insinuated that, because Tom had been married to her, he'd been a lucky man.

Her new husband was a man of few words and fewer smiles. He was belligerent and stubborn, and when he looked at her just so, she felt a tug on her insides and such a jumble of feelings she couldn't think straight.

Following him inside, she skirted him as if on eggshells. He'd removed his hat and had helped himself to the pitcher of orange juice in the refrigerator. Gliding her hands down the sides of her faded dress, she said, "Would you like some breakfast to go along with that?"

"I don't need a maid, Josie."

She did a double take all over again. "I...you...ugh." Bristling, she folded her arms with so much force she almost knocked the wind out of herself. "Fine," she finally managed. "Fix your own breakfast."

Since Jake had never cared who had the last word, he didn't bother answering. He strode to the stove and took down a frying pan hanging from a hook overhead. He could see into the living room from here, and although he tried not to, he found himself looking at the end stand where Tom's picture had been sitting early that morning. The table was bare except for a basket of wildflowers Josie must have picked while he'd been gone.

"Jake," Josie said, whisking the pan onto another burner and nudging him aside. "You might not need a maid, but if you keep this up, you're going to need the fire department. I enjoy cooking. Now what do you want?"

She jumped at the touch of his hand on her arm.

"What do I want?" he asked.

Both of his arms were suddenly around her, hauling her against the entire length of him. He was a hard man. It was what she'd expected. Steel and heat.

"I think you know what I want, Josie."

There was a hint of apology in his voice. Looking up at

him, she realized it was all the apology she was going to get.

"I want you." His voice was soft. That softness surprised her, tricked her into softening in return. His lips cajoled, his fingertips seeking out pleasure points, causing her to swoon. His hands went to her hips, lifting her right where he wanted her.

Oh, yes, she thought, tugging his shirt out of his jeans. It was a surprise and a trick. It was magic, and she reveled in it. All of it.

His shirt swished to the floor, the dress he claimed to loathe right behind it. The rest of their clothes followed, until they were naked and flushed and, finally, one.

They rode their passion to completion right there in the kitchen on the rug Muriel had just washed, a patch of sunlight filtering through the gleaming window, the breeze wafting through the screen door, the air rife with birdsong and the scent of coffee.

Some time later they picked through the clothing strewn around, Josie in her underwear, Jake in his jeans. "That," she muttered, "was certainly a first."

Handing her a thigh-high nylon in exchange for a work sock, Jake felt himself smile. First. He liked the sound of that.

Obviously flustered, she pulled on the rest of her clothes. "If I'm going to fix your breakfast, I'd better get to it. Kelsey will be wondering where I am. Now, would you like eggs? Pancakes?"

"Josie, wait."

She looked up from the stove, meeting his gaze.

"I had cold cereal with my coffee before I left the house. I'd like to go with you to get Kelsey. If you don't mind."

Mind? Josie couldn't even form a complete, coherent thought, let alone draw her wits about her enough to mind.

This hadn't happened to her when she'd been married to Tom. She and Tom had had a good marriage. Their sex life had been good, too. But it had never been like this. *She'd* never been like this.

Even in her befuddled state she knew it would only take a glance and a brush of fingertips and she would react all over again. Maybe she was reacting so strongly because she'd gone so long without being held. Or maybe she should stop trying to fool herself and give credit where credit was due. The sex had been incredible because Jake was incredible. Jake, who wasn't particularly sweet or kind. Jake, who had a good heart, a generous spirit, and…

"Well?" he prodded. "Are you coming or aren't you?"

…and an ornery disposition. Lord, what a combination. What a man.

Since he was already holding the door, she didn't bother answering. Feeling dazed and flustered, she concentrated on putting one foot in front of the other and simply strode through.

Chapter Eight

Kelsey bounced in her seat between Josie and Jake, talking a mile a minute. "Haley's eleven, but she said she
doesn't mind if I tag after her on accounta she's used to
her little brothers doing it."

"That's nice of her." Josie had said it quietly and, Jake
thought, a little absently. She'd been doing that a lot since
that episode in the kitchen. He'd thrown her off-kilter. He
rather liked it.

The radio had been tuned to a country-western station
during the ride to the Carson ranch. Now the radio was off,
and Kelsey filled the silence all by herself.

"Her daddy said he's gonna wash her mouth out with
soap if she doesn't stop swearing. I don't think it scared
her much. Nothing scares her. She can ride a horse real
good, and she thinks makeup is dumb. She keeps her room
real clean, but she didn't used to, and she makes Melody
laugh a lot. Just this morning she told Melody and Clayt
that she thinks boys are dumb, too, 'cept Jordan and Slade,
on accounta they're her brothers, and Logan Malone, on

accounta she's gonna marry him someday. Melody said she thought Clayt was gonna have a cow.''

Jake steered around a pothole in the road. He hadn't been around a lot of kids in his life, but this one was comical. She'd been chatting up a blue streak ever since they'd picked her up at the Carson ranch ten minutes ago. It was Haley, Jordan and Slade this, and Haley, Jordan and Slade that.

"All of them have horses," Kelsey exclaimed. "Even Slade, and he's not even two. And they have grandparents who live right next door to them. Do you have grandparents, Jake?"

Jake barely had time to shake his head before Kelsey rushed on. "I do, but Mama says they would have to use the jaws of life to pry open their wallets."

Jake's laughter started low in his throat, a rusty, crackly sound that erupted like a geyser at Yellowstone. He'd laughed more this past week than he had in the past six months put together. It was Josie's doing, and he had to admit, it felt good.

Kelsey hadn't come close to winding down when he pulled the truck beneath the Lone M sign out by the road. Barely waiting until he brought it to a stop close to the house, she scampered down from the truck and tugged on her mother's hand, only to release it and race ahead of them.

She was winded when they joined her inside, as if she'd made a quick pass through the first floor. Gliding across the kitchen, the little girl stooped down on the forest-green rug on the floor. "Look what I found, Mama."

Neither Jake nor Josie said anything as Josie accepted the little pearl earring from her daughter, but Jake felt himself heating up all over again. She'd been wearing two earrings when he'd first come in from the range. He couldn't pinpoint the exact moment one had come off, but he could narrow it down to one activity.

"I'm gonna go up to my room, Mama. You wanna come?"

"Maybe later." Josie watched the way her daughter dashed up the stairs. Glancing at the ceiling where the pitter-patter of small feet sounded overhead, she said, "I give her a day, two at the most, and she'll be sliding down that banister the way you said you used to."

"She's a cute kid. She's a dead ringer for her mother."

Why, that had almost sounded like a compliment. Josie turned to face Jake and found him looking at her, sexual intent written all over his face. It required concentration to keep from babbling. "She has my coloring, and Tom's eyes and personality. I probably shouldn't have told her that her grandparents are tight-fisted with their money. It's just that they make me so angry."

Jake's hand was warm on her arm and yet it raised goose bumps.

"No need to apologize. I know about anger. In fact, I could have written the book on it."

She felt herself warming, swaying toward him, his face blurring before her eyes as he lowered his mouth to hers. "Er, um, Jake?" she whispered.

"Hmm?" His face hovered mere inches from hers.

"There's something we haven't talked about."

There were a lot of things they hadn't talked about. There was good reason for that. He'd never felt less like talking in his life. Now if she wanted to know what he felt like doing, he would be happy to show her.

"It's important." She drew back a few inches.

Jake knew when he was licked. Josie had something important to say. Might as well stand back and let her say it. Besides, Kelsey was in the house, and he was going to have to wait to make love to his wife, anyway, so he straightened, too, giving her a little more room. "What haven't we talked about?"

"Protection."

The images of gunslingers and bank robbers flitted through his brain.

"You know," she whispered. "Birth control."

She had his undivided attention.

"Er, um, that is, we didn't use protection last night, or this morning, either. At the time I didn't give it a single thought."

"Neither one of us took time to do much thinking, Josie."

"Oh, I know. It's just that I got pregnant with Kelsey on my wedding night. I went on the pill after she was born, but then Tom died, and..."

Jake studied her quietly. She wasn't blushing, but her fingers were clasped tightly again, and Jake had a gut feeling that was making him damned uneasy.

"What I'm trying to say is everything's happened so fast. I'll make an appointment to see Dr. Kincaid as soon as possible, but in the meantime, I think we should use something else."

"You do." It wasn't a question.

Her eyes, wary now, met his. "Unless you'd prefer to wait the month it will take to be safe. Tom was thrilled to have a baby right away, but this situation is different..."

Jake felt a tightening in his throat and a chugging in his stomach. He was either having a heart attack or Josie had just blown a hole in his left ventricle. It was Tom. Always Tom.

Footsteps sounded on the stairs. They both turned just as Kelsey, lost in play, descended the stairs as regally as a princess. Kelsey, who, Josie had just said, had her mother's coloring and her *father's* personality. Kelsey, who had been conceived on Josie's wedding night.

Jake spun around, heading for the door and the peg where he kept his hat.

"Where ya going, Jake?" Kelsey called.

He came to an abrupt stop. Keeping his anger in check, he said, "I have work to do on the ranch."

The girl waltzed a little closer. "Haley said you and Mama are on your honeymoon, and honeymoons are like vacations, except with a lot more kissing."

"I guess you could call this a working honeymoon." Turning his attention to Josie, he said, "Muriel stocked the refrigerator, so there's plenty to eat. I don't know when I'll be back. There's no need to wait for me. And as far as the other...topic you mentioned, I'll take care of it. After all, we wouldn't want history to repeat itself."

He closed the door just short of a slam.

Jake sputtered for the best part of the next hour. Josie had the right to want to use protection. After all, she'd married him to keep her child, not to conceive another one. They hadn't discussed birth control. They sure as hell hadn't been thinking about it last night or this morning. She had every right to want to take care of herself, and he had no right to be angry.

And he wasn't angry. He lifted the hood of the Jeep and leaned over to take a look at the engine.

Heavens no. He wasn't angry. He was mad as hell.

She would see Doc Kincaid, she'd said. As soon as possible. Until then, they would need to use something else. Unless he preferred to wait the month it would take for her to be safe.

He'd gone a lot longer than that without sex. He could

wait. He could, dammit. He didn't need sex. He didn't need anything or anybody.

He yanked the dipstick out of the Jeep's engine with so much force he shoved his knuckles into the raised hood. Long before he'd finished the litany of cusswords ringing through his head, Sky ambled into the shed.

"I thought you were taking the rest of the day off, McKenna. What are you doing out here?"

He slammed the dip stick into place with a loud scrape. It served as Jake's reply.

Undeterred, Sky moseyed a little closer. "You and Josie looked pretty chummy a little while ago. So, how are things?"

Jake closed the hood. Giving Sky a wide berth, he strode to the driver's door.

"Where are you going?"

"Into Pierre for supplies."

"I thought you bought supplies last week."

Jake growled an answer, and Sky stood back to keep from getting run over.

Was that the door?

Josie stared at her reflection, absolutely, positively forbidding herself to take so much as one step out of this room to check. Heaven only knew she'd done it enough times already.

She wasn't lonely, she told herself. Jake had a ranch to run, and she had plenty to do. She didn't expect to be coddled. She knew how to take care of herself. She wasn't bored, either. She and Kelsey had taken a walk. They'd read stories. They'd had supper. She'd tucked her little girl into bed, and she'd taken a soothing, relaxing shower.

Footsteps thudded in the kitchen. Her hand stilled on the hairbrush, only to take up the task with so much renewed vigor her hair crackled. She paused when she heard the shower burst on down the hall. Very carefully she laid the brush down.

She wasn't bored. She wasn't lonely. She wasn't even angry. Well, not very angry, anyway. She was a fish out of water, that's what she was. In the span of one week, she'd closed her store, moved from her apartment and married a man she didn't understand.

She may have been shy, but she wasn't spineless. And she didn't take kindly to Jake's flashes from hot to cold. No, she didn't understand him, but she wasn't about to spend any more of her time trying to second-guess him. She had more important things to do. She could wash her car in the rain. Watch the grass grow. Count to a billion, backward.

Down the hall the pipes rumbled, and the shower was turned off. Nine hundred ninety-nine million nine hundred ninety-nine thousand nine hundred ninety-nine.

Jake entered the bedroom, his hair wet, a towel wrapped around his waist.

Nine hundred ninety-nine million nine hundred ninety-nine thousand nine hundred ninety-seven...

In his hand was a square box, the words Three Dozen on the side.

...or was that nine hundred ninety-eight?

He put the box on the nightstand, then walked toward her, all sinew, muscle and masculine grace, stopping so close to where she sat in front of the mirror she could feel the heat emanating from his body. There was heat in his eyes, too, and a seriousness she didn't understand any more than she understood him.

He placed his hands over his head in a casual stretch. He wasn't fooling her. There was nothing casual about him.

"What are you doing, Jake?" she asked, her gaze on his through the mirror.

"I'm not so difficult to understand." His lips were moist and hot on her cheek, his hand big and rough, his chest solid. She practically floated to her feet. He turned her and kissed her. Not in the wild, frenzied way she'd expected, but tenderly, and so sweetly she nearly cried out.

He was wrong. He *was* difficult to understand. Impossible. She didn't have a clue what went on in the deep, dark recesses of his mind. She never knew what he was going to do next. She certainly never understood why he did what he did.

"I made a little trip into Pierre."

She felt her eyebrows rise. Maybe she understood *that*. Glancing at the nightstand, she said, "Three dozen, Jake? Is that a week's supply?"

He didn't smile, and she found herself wanting him to, almost as much as she wanted him to kiss her again. His hands went to the front of her robe. Moments later it fluttered to the floor along with his towel.

"A week's supply," he whispered, lowering her to the bed. "You underestimate me, Josephine."

Threading her fingers through his damp hair, she shook her head and smiled. His subtle humor surprised her and reinforced the fact that she simply didn't understand him. Maybe she should rethink her earlier stand about trying to figure him out. His hand glided across her stomach. Mmm. Yes, she would try to understand him. Later. Much, much later.

"Me and Breanna and Alyssa were playing tag when that mean TaylorAnne Shultz tried to push me down on accounta she didn't want me to play with *her* friends. Breanna and Alyssa are nice, but TaylorAnne isn't. She says I'm ugly and my old clothes are the ugliest of all."

"That wasn't very nice of TaylorAnne," Josie said, turning onto Old Stump Road.

Kelsey pulled a face. "She says I used to be poor, but now that you married Jake, we're rich. Is that true, Mama?"

Josie glanced at the herd of cattle grazing on the horizon, considering her reply. She'd purchased new clothes for Kelsey with the money Jayne Stryker had paid her for subletting the store. She didn't want Kelsey to think clothes made the person.

"Does TaylorAnne wear nice clothes, Kelsey?"

Kelsey nodded her head so hard the ribbon came out of her hair. "She wears dresses mostly. Pretty ones. And she's always telling us how much they cost. They're never on sale."

Josie hid a smile. The Schultzes had TaylorAnne long after they'd given up hope of having children. Mrs. Schultz was nice enough, but she put her only child up on a pedestal, indulging her daughter to the point of spoiling her.

"Do you think TaylorAnne is happy?"

"Happy?" Kelsey asked.

"Yes. You know, does she smile, laugh, have fun?"

Kelsey shook her head. "She's bossy and she's mean, and most times she looks like this." Kelsey's face contorted into a pinched, exaggerated scowl.

"That's a shame," Josie said. "I've always thought a smile was a person's inner beauty shining through to the outside."

Kelsey skewed her mouth up, pondering the notion. Mother and daughter both noticed the man sitting on the fence out by the corral in the distance, but Kelsey pointed, saying, "There's Jake, Mama."

"Mmm-hmm."

"He doesn't smile much, but he's not ugly, is he, Mama?"

Josie very nearly stammered. Leave it to her darling daughter to blow a hole in the point she'd been trying to make. "No, Kelsey. Jake isn't ugly at all. In fact, he's one of the most ruggedly attractive men I've ever met."

Kelsey giggled at that. They continued to talk as Josie pulled into the driveway. "Girl talk" was what Josie's mother used to call it.

"Hi, Jake," Kelsey called, pushing out of the door, her backpack forgotten. "Guess what? Mama says being pretty ain't all on the outside, and that I've got it comin' and goin'. And she said you're the most ruggably—" The girl turned to her mother. "What did you call it, Mama?"

Josie picked her way around the back of the car, carefully meeting Jake's gaze before eyeing her precocious daughter. "I believe the term I used was ruggedly attractive, sweet pea."

Jake was looking at her when she turned her attention back to him. Her declaration won her the first smile of the day, which drew her gaze to Jake's mouth. A serious mistake for a woman who was trying valiantly not to blush.

"That a fact?" he said quietly.

"And guess what?" Kelsey quipped, oblivious to the sudden change in atmosphere. "Mrs. Carson let me ring the bell for recess. She has red hair, too. What's in the basket, Jake?"

For the first time, Josie noticed the picnic basket sitting at Jake's feet. "Buck and Billy are checking on the herd north of here. And Sky and Slappy are riding fences to the west. Since it hasn't rained in a week, the current in Sugar Creek should be slow and the water clear. I had Muriel pack us a lunch, and I thought maybe the three of us could take a little drive and maybe have an early picnic supper.''

He bent at the waist, picking up the basket with one hand, pushing up the brim of his hat with the other. Josie's breath hitched. Ruggedly attractive didn't even begin to cover the way he looked. Jake McKenna had the looks, the style and, oh, yes, the moves, to unsettle a feminine heart. And unsettle her is what he did. This wasn't the first time it had happened. Helping Kelsey into the Jeep, Josie hoped it wouldn't be the last.

She and Jake had been married for a week and a half. Their days had settled into a routine of sorts. Jake put in long hours on the ranch. Kelsey caught the bus to school, and Josie spent her days planting flowers and doing what she could to turn the big house into a home. Sometimes she picked Kelsey up from school, and the two of them spent the remainder of the afternoon together. Jake joined them for supper most nights, going back to work, only to return sometime between dusk and midnight. He'd introduced them both to the horses, and was even teaching Kelsey to ride. Although he didn't smile often, he treated Josie's little girl with kindness, answering the dozens of questions she asked with a degree of patience Josie hadn't known he possessed.

Jake wasn't an easy man to know. What an understatement. There were layers to his personality, some of them buried deep and covered by stone. Sometimes she felt like an excavator at an ancient dig, sifting through dirt, chiseling away at clues one chip at a time. At this rate it was going to take years for Josie to discover all the pieces that made up Jake's personality.

They bounced over the rough terrain, following the narrow lane south and then east. "Are we almost there?" Kelsey asked. "Cuz I'm starving. Slappy says I must have a hollow leg. Do you think I have a hollow leg, Mama?"

"You don't have a hollow leg, Kelsey."

She placed her hand over her heart as if she'd been taking lessons from Brandy Schafer. "What a relief."

They spread a blanket on the grassy area near the bank of Sugar Creek. After eating her fill of fried chicken, potato salad and crusty bread, Kelsey crept down the bank where the creek was wide but less than a foot deep. Josie and Jake joined her at the water's edge, the three of them yelping and Kelsey giggling as they tried to catch frogs. It was so simple and yet so much fun, the most fun Josie had had in a long time.

Kelsey fell asleep during the ride home. It must have relaxed Jake, too, because for once, he opened up a little, talking about how life on the ranch had been when he was a young boy. "Cole and I used to sneak down to the creek every chance we got. We used to fish, catch frogs, float cucumber boats downstream until they sank."

"It sounds nice," Josie said, picturing it in her mind. "I always wanted a brother or a sister."

Jake nodded. "I thought the sun rose and set on Cole's shoulders. Even though I was four years younger, he let me go everywhere he went. Except one day when Betty Jean Nelson happened to stop by. Isaac was at a cattle auction in Sioux Falls, so Cole and I were on our own. When Cole and Betty Jean started for the creek, I started after them. Cole gave me strict instructions to stay put. I did, too, for about ten minutes. And then I sneaked after them. I was real quiet, right up until I fell out of the tree I'd climbed to get a better look at Betty Jean without her shirt. I broke my arm and darn near broke my neck."

"Oh, Jake, you didn't."

He glanced at Kelsey, who was sound asleep on Josie's lap. "I did. Betty Jean was well endowed for fifteen."

Josie laughed. "I meant you didn't really break your arm falling out of a tree."

"That, too. My arm healed, but I've been partial to shirtless women ever since."

Of all times for him to smile. Josie shook her head, but she smiled in return. It was the closest they'd come to bantering, and her heart swelled with feeling. It hurt a little around the edges, happiness, because she knew how quickly it could turn into sadness. That didn't stop her from feeling it, from reveling in it. And it didn't stop her from wanting Jake to feel it, too.

They drove the remainder of the way in silence, Garth serenading them over the radio. She didn't pretend to know what Jake was thinking, but at least she felt that she knew him a little better, understood him a little more than she had a few hours ago. It was a start.

The last pothole roused Kelsey out of her sleep. Her head popped up and she resumed talking as if she'd never stopped. "Look, Bommer and King are waiting for their treats."

"Be careful, Kelsey," Josie said. "Horses have been known to nip little girls' fingers along with the sugar cubes."

"Jake showed me how to hold my hand real flat and keep my fingers tight together."

Watching Kelsey run to the fence to offer the big geldings something sweet, Josie said, "You're good with her."

"She's not a hard kid to be good to."

"She likes it here."

"What about you, Josie? Do you like it here?"

Josie stared up at her husband's face. There were squint lines beside his eyes, the shadow of a day-old beard on his cheeks and jaw, angles and planes and contours that made him unique and handsome, but it was the glint in his eyes that set her heart aflutter. Redistributing her weight to one foot, she cocked her head and practically batted her eyelashes. "I'm learning my way around."

His eyes darkened as if he was enjoying the mild flirtation. Staring at the horizon where McKenna land met with the sky, he said, "I have to go back out. I'll take the Jeep." He started for the shed. Turning at the waist, he glanced back at her. "It rides hard, but it'll get me there and back faster."

Most of the time Josie didn't pretend to understand him, but it didn't take a genius to read between those lines. If she had been a little more bold, she would have reminded him that he'd once told her that *hard* and *fast* should never be used in the same sentence.

She pulled her gaze from his masculine swagger, turning her attention to her daughter, her thoughts already racing ahead to his return.

Jake pulled his truck to a stop near the barn and opened the door, his eyes searching for a movement or a glimpse of pale fabric or a flash of light red hair. It had been four days since that picnic down by the creek. Four very sexy, incredible, enjoyable days.

Muriel claimed a change had come over him. Just yesterday she'd told him that marriage seemed to be agreeing with him. Snitching a sliver of ham from the cutting board directly in front of her, Jake had said, "Not you, too. Last night Slappy said the same thing, only he worded it a little differently. I think he said something about sex and supper and how they were working wonders with my disposition."

Jake had gotten his hand slapped and his ears reamed. "Why, there's more to marriage than home-cooked meals and sharing your bed with a warm and willing woman. Leave it to that crass old cowpoke to try to tell you differently. Why, that man wouldn't know class if it bit him in the butt. I swear he tries to irritate me."

Muriel rambled on, and Jake's mind had wandered. Was there more to marriage? he'd wondered. He hoped not, because this was all he had to offer, all he dared hope for. For a moment a sense of dread had climbed up his spine. He'd squelched it, concentrating instead on the splotch of color on Muriel's lined cheeks and the starry glint in her eyes. He'd heard plenty of women sputter about plenty of men, but in his experience, when a woman's eyes went all dewy the way Muriel's had, there was usually more to the story.

Slappy and Muriel. Well, well, well.

He didn't want to think about Slappy and Muriel as he scanned the porch, the driveway where Josie's old sedan was parked and finally the yard. He sure as hell didn't want to think about the sense of dread that had hovered over him all his life. But it was there, even as a zing went through him the instant he found what he'd been looking for. Tamping down the dread, he removed his hat, raked his fingers through his hair and started toward the side yard where Josie had been digging and hoeing for days.

She didn't jump when his shadow flickered across the rich soil at her feet. She was accustomed to his unscheduled visits during the day.

"Hi." She sounded breathless.

He took a step closer. Ah, this was better, he thought, a sensation much more pleasing than agitation and dread heating his body and his thoughts.

"If you came back for your rope," she said, putting her weight into the short jabs she made with the hoe, "I think I saw it in the barn earlier."

She was wearing jeans today, faded and so worn they hugged her hips and rear like a second skin. He liked her in jeans, but not as much as he liked her out of them.

"I don't need my rope, Josie."

Her hair covered the side of her face, blocking his view of her mouth, but he thought her voice held a smile when she said, "I try not to look at the branding irons and syringes and the horse pills you give those poor cattle."

Yes. Her voice was definitely smiling.

"So I don't know where they are, but if it's a jug of water you want, Muriel would be happy to get it for you."

His third step was much shorter than the first two had been. "Muriel's here again today?"

She glanced at him, and he saw that her voice wasn't the only part of her that was smiling. "I think there's something going on between her and Slappy. Her son dropped her off this morning, saying something about her car needing repairs." She went back to her hoeing. "Muriel is a lovely woman. Bossy, maybe, but she has a good heart and a lot of pride."

Jake wondered why she was telling him something he already knew. *Patience,* the voice inside his head whispered. *She'll get to it if you give her a chance.*

Jake clamped his mouth shut. Everyone knew patience wasn't his long suit. Somebody ought to tell that annoying voice in his head.

As if oblivious to his sudden vexation, Josie said, "When you first told me you'd hired a woman from town to come out twice a week to cook and clean, I assumed I would take over after we were married."

"I didn't marry you to do the cooking and cleaning, Josie."

Josie didn't bother bristling. She knew why he'd married

her. Originally, at least. Lately she thought he was glad for more reasons than one.

"I would have been happy to do all the cooking and cleaning, but Muriel is living on a fixed income, and I've gathered that she needs the money you pay her. I've thoroughly enjoyed having the opportunity to garden and spend so much time with Kelsey, but I think it's time for me to look for a job."

"What kind of job?"

Two lines had formed in Jake's forehead, causing Josie to choose her words carefully. "I can do most anything. Office work, retail, waitressing. Anything that earns honest pay."

"Honest pay."

He was repeating her words again. She'd learned that he did that when he didn't particularly like what she was saying. "I have bills, Jake. I wouldn't feel right letting you pay them."

He gave her a narrow, piercing glance. "I have the money, Josie."

"I can't take it."

"Why the hell not?"

"Because, if I did, Gretchen and Charles would be right."

"I don't give a rip what Charles and Gretchen think."

She held up a hand, silencing whatever else he was going to say. "What about the people of Jasper Gulch, Jake? Do you care what they think? Because I do. I won't have people saying that Kelsey Callahan's mother is a gold digger."

The lines in his forehead deepened, and he had to unclench his teeth in order to speak. "I thought Jayne Stryker paid you the first and last month's rent for the store."

"She did. I have other expenses."

"Other expenses."

"Yes. Debts."

"Debts."

He was repeating her words again. She had to fight to keep from rolling her eyes in exasperation. "Yes, debts, Jake. Hospital expenses. And funeral expenses. Tom and I didn't have insurance."

Jake's expression reminded her of a cloud passing before the sun. His eyes were suddenly hooded, his face difficult to read. He took a backward step, removed his hat, shoved his fingers through his hair, then crammed his hat back on his head. As far as indicators went, it was a pretty good one. He was angry. She didn't know why.

"You don't want me to work?" she asked cautiously.

"It's a free country. You're free to get a job or do whatever you want. The Jeep blew a tire. If I don't get going, Sky's going to start walking back to the bunkhouse."

She watched Jake speed toward the shed where he kept his truck. Intuition told her he would have preferred to heave a saddle onto King's broad back and go for a hard, fast ride.

He was angry. Why? she asked herself. He was a proud man. Surely he understood her pride and her desire to put Tom's expenses behind her.

She returned to her task, but not before she made a solemn vow to find out what had brought the shutters to his eyes and the anger that kept him closed off from her and the rest of the world.

Chapter Nine

"Mama?"

"Yes, sweet pea?" Josie said, taking the last pan of cookies from the oven.

"Is Jake my daddy now?"

The cookie sheet clattered to the stove. Kelsey was looking at her, her little fingers gripping a blue crayon. Josie had known the question was coming. After all, Kelsey had been asking for a new father for a long time.

Transferring the hot cookies from the pan to a clean kitchen towel, Josie took care to keep her voice casual and even as she said, "Technically Jake is your stepfather."

"Melody is Haley's stepmother," Kelsey said matter-of-factly. "Sometimes she calls her Mom. Do you think Jake would mind if I called him Daddy?"

Josie's heart thudded and her chest ached. Kelsey was a bright, inquisitive little girl. She was bound to want what all children wanted. A home and two parents who loved her. Josie understood Kelsey's yearning for a father. Her own father had died when she was eight. Her mother had seen to it that she'd had a happy childhood. She'd always known her mama had loved her, but she remembered sitting on the trailer steps, watching the neighborhood fathers come home from work. They had deep voices and big hands. They fiddled with engines, fell asleep in their chairs and didn't mind getting dirty. Most of them were nice to her, but none of them ever told her to call him Daddy.

Jake also had a deep voice and big hands and didn't mind getting dirty. He'd been good to Kelsey, but before Kelsey got any more attached, Josie had to talk to him.

She'd vowed to do it last night. At the time it had seemed like a good strategy. There was one problem with that plan. Jake McKenna wasn't an easy man to talk to. It didn't help that he was out on the range so much of the time. He'd come in for supper last night. Although he'd said please and thank you, he'd remained pensive and aloof and completely unapproachable. He'd arrived back home after she'd already been asleep, and had left again in the wee hours of the morning before she'd awakened. He'd been there. The covers were messed, and his scent had been on his pillow. He'd slept in their bed, but he hadn't reached for her. It was the first time since they'd exchanged wedding vows nearly two weeks ago.

He and his men had come and gone throughout the day. She'd caught glimpses of them near the bunkhouse and barn. The crunch of tires on the driveway, the rumble of an engine, the low murmur of their voices had drifted to her ears from time to time. Billy had spun out of the driveway a little while ago, Buck a few minutes behind him.

Turning off the oven, she went to the window. Jake and Sky were deep in conversation out by the corral. More determined than ever to snag a few minutes of Jake's time, she told Kelsey she would be right back, and headed outside.

Although Sky was the first to swipe his hat off his head and slant her a big old smile, he wasn't the only one who noticed her approach. He was, however, the only one who spoke. "Afternoon, Josie."

"Hi, Sky." Josie liked Skyler Buchanan. He had an infectious grin and a legendary swagger. He gave the impression of a footloose and fancy-free cowboy. Josie had seen the way he rode up the lane at breakneck speed, toying with fate and throwing caution to the wind, and she happened to believe there was more to him than he would have folks believe. She didn't understand what drove him, but who was she to question him? She was having enough trouble trying to understand Jake. Which brought her to the reason she'd come outside.

"The flowers look good, Josie," Sky said.

She shot him a quick glance. "Thanks."

"I was just telling Jake here that there's nothing like a woman to pretty a place up a little. Isn't that right, Jake?"

Jake regarded his friend for a moment. Josie might not have recognized the mocking glint in Sky's eyes, but Jake sure did. What Sky had really been asking was why in the hell Jake was spending so much time out here when he had a wife as pretty as Josie waiting inside.

That was a good question. The truth was, he didn't know the answer. It had to do with control, and with the sense of yearning mixed with dread that wrapped around his windpipe every time he caught a glimpse of her. It had only been a few days since he'd held her, but his body was reacting to the sight, the sound, the knowledge that she was nearby this very instant.

He wanted her. So what? He was a grown man, and he could control his most basic instincts. That's what back-breaking work and exhaustion were for. Jake didn't mind hard work, and he liked to be in control. Control put a man on solid ground.

"Trouble?"

It was Josie's voice, and it took him a full five seconds to comprehend the fact that she was referring to the truck that had pulled into the driveway.

"That's Luke Carson," Jake said.

"He's the local veterinarian," Sky added.

"I know who Luke Carson is," Josie said quietly. "Is something wrong with some of the animals?"

Jake and Sky gave a quick rundown of the potential problem Sky had spotted with the small herd of cattle grazing out in the south pasture. "It might just be bloat," Jake said.

"Let's hope it's just bloat." Sky's voice held a ring of impending doom.

Luke Carson joined them, and the three men started for Jake's truck.

"Jake?"

Sky and Luke glanced at her absently, only to resume the conversation they were having in hushed tones. Jake stopped completely and turned around.

"I know you're worried about the cattle, so I won't hold you up, but I was wondering, hoping really..."

Jake's attention strayed to the way the wind toyed with her hair and fluttered the collar of her faded dress. All the hard work in the world couldn't have kept him from reacting, from remembering, from wanting.

"Yes?" he asked, more gruffly than he'd intended.

She seemed to be having as much trouble concentrating as he was. With a slight shake of her head she said, "There's something we need to talk about. It's important. I'll be waiting."

They turned in opposite directions, Josie heading for the

house. Jake lengthened his stride until he caught up with Sky and Luke. The men walked abreast, all three of them tall, all three of them broad. Jake was the only one who felt as if he was about to stumble off solid ground.

It was long past supper time when Jake returned to the house. The smell of pepper steak and gravy was still heavy on the air. He washed up at the deep sink in the laundry room. Drying his hands on a threadbare towel he didn't recognize, he strode into the kitchen. His place was still set, but the rest of the dishes had been cleared away. There was a crayon drawing on the counter. Jake studied what appeared to be a stick woman, a stick child and half of a stick man.

He strode to the oven, leaned over and peered inside. His stomach rumbled. Turning the oven off, he reached for a pot holder just as two feminine voices filtered through the closed bathroom door.

"Can I add more bubbles, Mama?"

"No more bubbles. If you stay in this bathtub any longer, you'll turn into a prune. See? Your toes already look like raisins."

Kelsey giggled. And Jake almost smiled. He'd gotten his feet back underneath him, so to speak, out on the range. There was nothing like a brush with disaster to put things in perspective. He'd finally figured out why he'd felt like climbing the wall. He'd been avoiding Josie because she brought out needs he hadn't known he still had. It was as if there was something buried deep inside him. It made him feel like a little kid yearning for his mother's touch.

He didn't need a mother, dammit. He hadn't in a long time. His need for Josie was different. He didn't like needing, but he'd put it in perspective this afternoon while he'd been out on the range. He equated needing with control, or a lack of control. He'd had no control over Nadine's desertion or Cole's death or Isaac's callousness. He wasn't a little boy anymore. Hadn't been in a long, long time. He was a grown man. A married man. As long as he kept his yearning in the bedroom, everything would be all right.

From the other side of the bathroom door came the splash of water, the scrape of a cupboard door, the thud of two small feet hopping to the floor. He opened the oven door a little farther and reached for the plate warming on the middle shelf. He removed the upside-down bowl and thought about carrying his dinner to the table. The aroma overtook him, and he ended up taking his first bite where he stood.

Sex and supper, Slappy had said, worked wonders on a man's disposition. Jake couldn't have agreed more. That wife of his was a darn good cook. Now that he'd had some time to think things through, he planned to partake in the other half of that recipe for happiness as soon as possible.

"Do you think Jake will come home before I go to bed?" Kelsey's voice carried through the closed door.

"It's hard to say, sweet pea. This is a busy time of year on a ranch."

There were a series of clunks and then Kelsey asked, "Did you ask him yet?"

Jake stopped chewing.

"Did ya? Did you ask him if it's okay for me to call him Daddy?"

A shudder went through Jake, squeezing into his chest from the inside. He didn't move, not even to breathe. Although he listened with all his might, he couldn't quite make out Josie's reply.

He started when the door opened. By the time Josie noticed him standing in the middle of the kitchen, he'd recovered and was making a dent in the mashed potatoes and gravy on the plate in his hand.

"Jake. I didn't know you were back."

"I just came in."

"Hi, Jake!"

She'd called him Jake, not Daddy. "Hi, Kels."

"Mama says I don't hafta go to bed until my hair dries and I can watch TV. You wanna watch it with me?"

It was Josie who answered. "Jake's eating."

"Oh." The little girl looked him up and down. "Are you gonna ask him right now, Mama?"

Jake met Josie's stare head-on. Yes, he thought, issuing a silent challenge.

"Kelsey, honey, I don't think..."

Jake silenced Josie with a step in her direction. "What is it you wanted to ask me?"

"How are the cattle?"

"The cattle?"

Kelsey rolled her eyes. "No, Mama, not the cattle." Turning to Jake, the little girl said, "I was wonderin'." She stopped, peered at her pink toes, than started again. "I mean, I was hopin'..."

Her second pause put Jake in mind of her mother. She took a step toward him and looked up at him, all in one motion. In a voice suddenly gone shy she said, "Would you run the three-legged race with me at the family picnic on the last day of school?"

"The three-legged race?"

"I'm sure Jake would like to go with you, sweet pea—with us," Josie said in a rush, "but this is a big ranch and a busy time of the year and he might not—"

"I'd like that, Kels."

Josie's and Kelsey's heads both jerked upward. "You would?" Josie asked.

"You will?" Kelsey said at the same time.

Jake nodded his head one time before turning his attention back to his supper. Kelsey clapped her hands, danced a little jig, then retired to the living room to watch her favorite television program.

All at once the kitchen was quiet. Too quiet. Josie could hear the clink of Jake's fork on his plate, the rustle of denim as he settled his hips more comfortably against the counter, the crinkle of his boots as he crossed his ankles.

"Earlier you mentioned that there was something important you wanted to talk to me about," he said, spearing a baby green bean. "Now's as good a time as any."

He'd spoken without looking at her. Josie was relieved. It gave her the opportunity to get her thoughts in order. The family fun day at school had been part of what she'd wanted to discuss. It had been nice of him to agree to go, but it was too soon to talk about the far-reaching future. Just how did a woman go about asking the man she'd married out of mutual need how long he thought the union would last? Neither of them had mentioned forever. Perhaps it would be best to take things in smaller increments.

"Running the three-legged race with you will mean a lot to Kelsey."

He stopped eating and looked at her, the expression in his eyes one she couldn't decipher. If only she knew him better, knew what he was thinking, feeling.

He shrugged. "She's a cute kid."

"Thank you. Although it wasn't really my doing."

Jake's heartbeat slowed. He remembered when Josie had told him Kelsey had her coloring and Tom's eyes and personality. Come on, Josie, he thought, ask me to be a father to that little girl. Bury Tom once and for all. Take the next step.

Her gaze flickered to him, then away, then back again.

"Is something wrong, Josephine?"

"Oh. No. Not really. Well. It's just that Kelsey likes you. Very much. And she was, well, she was hoping…"

"Yes?"

She seemed to get a hold of herself. She stopped fidgeting, and she stopped stammering, and she met his gaze evenly. "She would like it very much if you would read her a story sometime. And…"

Jake took a step toward her, the low drone of the television in the next room the only sound covering the wild thump of his heart.

"And I know you're busy, and I don't want to impose, but she would love to spend more time with you." Josie clamped her mouth shut. There. She'd made the first move toward paving the way for a relationship between Jake and Kelsey. Now she prayed Jake would respond.

He was staring at her so hard she wondered if he might crawl right inside her, but he wasn't saying anything. Josie bit her lip, fidgeted with her watch, picked at her fingernail. Grasping the first thought to flit into her head, she said, "I circled some want ads in the paper. At least I have a few leads. Did you get enough to eat? What was wrong with those cattle, by the way?"

Jake placed his empty plate and fork in the sink. She'd failed to relay Kelsey's desire to call him Daddy. She was searching for a job when he could have paid off those stinking bills of hers with one check. And she wanted to talk about the cattle?

He ran a hand over his face. Aw, hell. "Luke thinks they got hold of some locoweed somewhere. We sprayed last year, but unless you get it all, the darn stuff comes back. The cattle didn't eat enough to kill them, but they aren't feeling too good right now. Problem with cattle is they have short memories. They'll forget all about how sick they are right now and eat locoweed all over again first chance they get. I can certainly relate. Follow me.''

He'd muttered the last part while he was walking away from Josie, causing her to wonder if she'd heard him right. What did he mean he could relate?

She followed him into a room Muriel had referred to as Old Isaac's study. Jake opened a closet and from a high shelf retrieved two shoe boxes filled with receipts. He went to a large desk next. "If you're good with numbers, and it's work you're looking for," he said, handing her a stack of files, papers spilling out of every side, "I could use a hand with the accounting."

Josie eyed the thick folders, the crinkled receipts, the scribbled writing. Her eyebrows went up, because from the looks of things, he needed a dozen extra hands.

She imagined the ledgers she would fill, the numbers she would post, the sums she would total. She warmed to the challenge, invigorated by the idea of all those blessed numbers. She liked numbers. They were tangible, honest, unflappable. You could depend on numbers. A three was always a three. No matter how many ways a hundred was divided, if you put it back together, it was still a hundred in the end.

She paused, growing serious. There was one downfall. "I don't know, Jake."

"What now?"

"I would feel funny taking money from you."

He swore under his breath. "I can either pay an accountant or pay you. Suit yourself."

His voice was gruff. Yes, Jake McKenna was much more difficult to understand than numbers. "How much would you want to pay me?"

He shrugged in an offhand way and casually named a figure.

Her mouth dropped open. "That's a lot of money."

"That's a lot of work. My father went through accountants the way dogs go through bones. Nobody could get along with him well enough to stick around. I've managed to keep the men and bills paid and the checkbook balanced. I've had to let everything else slide. It's the going rate, Josie. Do we have a deal or don't we?"

She glanced at the folders and receipts, imagining the hours she could spend lost in debits and credits, not to mention the money she would be able to put toward Tom's final expenses. Smiling, she stuck out her hand. "We have a deal."

Jake eyed her hand, and before she could do more than gasp, he took it, and her along with it, hauling her into his arms, his mouth covering hers. Her breath caught, and a sound only she could hear echoed deep in her chest.

The kiss was over as quickly as it began. Jake was halfway to the door before she'd gathered her wits enough to ask, "Where are you going?"

He looked at her over his shoulder, and it occurred to her that he wasn't nearly as shaken as she was. With maddening male logic he said, "I have to take some salt licks out by the water hole in the west pasture."

"Will you be late?"

"Do you want me to be late?"

Of all the arrogant, self-centered... She shook her head.

Jake's breath rushed out of him. Being wanted by Josie was a heady sensation. It sent powerful emotions through him and nearly buckled his knees. It was all he could do to keep from rushing right back to her and saying to hell with the herd. His pride held him in place. "I'll be back as quickly as I can."

He left the house the same way he'd entered, his stride

gaining strength and speed. Yes sir, he had his feet back underneath him and he was walking on solid ground.

Josie poked her head inside the living room. The television was on, Kelsey's dress-up dolls naked and forgotten on top of their clothes, but Kelsey was nowhere to be found. Josie checked the back porch next, Kelsey's bedroom and finally the kitchen. Where had her little girl wandered off to?

A high-pitched twitter carried to her ears through the screen in the kitchen. Josie went to the window, smiling at the sheer joy in her daughter's laughter.

It had been two weeks since Jake had turned the books over to her, two weeks since he'd started spending more time with Kelsey. Her heart had nearly swelled to bursting the first time she'd heard him read to her little girl. Kelsey was happy. Happier than she'd been in a long time.

Josie was the one who was lonely.

She touched her finger to the pointy top of the cheap trophy Jake and Kelsey had won for taking first place in the three-legged race yesterday. This wasn't so bad, this life she was living now. She had everything she needed here. A daughter who was smart and charming and sometimes conniving. A roof over their heads. Three meals a day, and an income, a means to repay her debt.

This wasn't so bad. She had everything she needed. Except a man to share everything she needed with.

It wasn't that Jake did anything wrong. He treated her with respect. He picked up after himself. He'd practically gushed with praise for the job she was doing with the books for the Lone M. He was ardent and passionate in bed. But he was also quiet. Sometimes she found him watching her, and she wanted to go to him and ask him what he was thinking. Ultimately he would turn away, or ride off in the

Jeep or on his horse, and she would have to face the fact that she was no closer to knowing him than she'd been before they'd wed.

They said old habits died hard and that you couldn't teach an old dog new tricks. Maybe things would have been different if they'd started talking in the beginning. But they'd never been completely open with each other. And it seemed they didn't know how to start now.

Kelsey laughed again. This time it was followed by the deep, rolling sound of Jake's rusty laughter. Josie's gaze followed the sound. Jake was hunkered down in the side yard not far from the hollyhocks and day lilies she'd planted. His jeans stretched taut across his thighs, his dusty black Stetson pushed up in the front, a look of rapt attention on his face as he listened to whatever Kelsey was saying.

Turning away from the scene, Josie swallowed the lump in her throat. Everything was going to be all right. Jake had said it himself. No judge in his right mind would ever take that child away from Josie now. Any fool could see she was happy.

Kelsey's happiness was enough. It was.

Josie wavered. All right. She would make it be enough. And by God, she would be happy, too.

"We've gotta move the herd away from the eastern boundary and we've gotta do it soon." Slappy spit, and Jake squinted in the late-morning sunshine.

"They're eatin' all the way to the dirt, just like they always do. Gluttons, that's what they are," Slappy continued.

"It would help if it would rain. It's dryer than a witches whistle out there." This time it was Sky's voice cutting into Jake's reverie.

"It's early to be this dry," Jake said absently.

"Darn right it's early. If it keeps this up, we'll be moving the herd to Sugar Creek by the end of July."

"Here come Buck and Billy," Sky said.

Jake's younger two hired hands were approaching the lane at a gallop, their horses stirring up a cloud of dust that hung in the uncommonly still air. In comparison, the area surrounding the big house looked lush. Baskets of flowers hung from the porch. More flowers bloomed in clay pots on the steps and along the sidewalk. There was even a vine of something starting to climb the pole holding the birdhouse Josie and Kelsey had made.

"Do you, Jake?"

He turned his head slowly. "Hmm?"

Sky and Slappy both eyed him strangely. "Want us to round up Buck and Billy and ride out there today?"

He muttered an answer. He wondered where Josie was.

"...on over to the western slope. You okay, Jake?"

"What? Oh. Couldn't be better." Jake forced his attention to his men, only to lose his concentration all over again at the sound of feminine laughter that seemed to carry for miles on the still, dry air. "Excuse me for a minute or two boys."

Sky and Slappy watched him from underneath their worn cowboy hats. "No matter what that boy says," Slappy grumbled to Sky. "Everything ain't all right. I hope I'm a ways away when he figures that out."

Watching his friend, Sky hoped the smile Jake swore was real didn't blow up in his face.

Jake could feel their eyes on him. Since there was no law against looking, he didn't say anything. But he commended himself on his control.

He'd thought he'd heard laughter coming from the house. He listened intently, but he was pretty sure he was alone. Josie's touches were everywhere, in the vases of wildflowers on a windowsill, in the pie cooling on the counter, in the frilly doily on the table, the chipped teacup holding the stones Kelsey had collected, the child's artwork on the refrigerator. He found himself in their bedroom, staring at the big bed where they made love nearly every night. For some reason he went to Josie's closet. All her inexpensive faded dresses were there, along with a few pairs of practical shoes.

Blasted, stubborn woman refused to buy new clothes, even though he'd paid her the last four weeks for keeping the ranch's books. He turned all of a sudden and traipsed into Isaac's study. The old desk was tidy, papers stacked in neat piles, brightly colored file folders held together with a big rubber band. He opened the top drawer. Pens and sharpened pencils filled the front tray. Directly behind them was a statement bearing the name of a hospital in Mississippi. He picked it up. Underneath it was the framed photo Josie had clutched to her breast the night Jake married her.

Something restless and unwelcome stirred inside him. He tamped it down and studied the statement from the hospital. It bore Monday's date. Every dime Josie had earned doing the Lone M's books was present and accounted for. Every dime had gone to pay for her beloved Tom's hospital expenses.

The paper crinkled in Jake's fisted hand. Loosening his grip, he returned the itemized list to the drawer and closed it tight.

Kelsey's laughter carried to his ears again. He followed the sound to the window overlooking the backyard. Kelsey and Josie were there, butterfly nets in their hands. They were both wearing gauzy, yellow dime-store dresses, their red hair billowing behind them in their play. A yearning to join them washed over Jake. He closed his eyes, turned on his heel and joined Sky and Slappy in the barn.

Jake McKenna was still in control.

Chapter Ten

Josie was laughing when she hung up the phone. She'd heard the door open and was a little surprised to find Jake standing near it, watching her. Her laughter faded, but she was still smiling as she said, "That was Melody Carson. Honestly, she says the funniest things. She wants to know if we'd like to come to their party on the Fourth of July."

He remained near the door. His cowboy hat sat low on his forehead, and he was looking at her as if he liked what he saw. Still, he didn't come any closer. It reminded her a little of the way Lisa McCully had looked at a cookie when she'd been trying to lose those last five pounds after her daughter was born.

Josie didn't understand why he held back. After all, when he looked at her like that, she melted, and he could have anything he wanted.

"Where's Kels?"

"She's upstairs pouting because I wouldn't let her watch any more television. Do you want me to call her?"

"No." He finally took a few steps toward her. "I think I should run this by you before…"

What sounded like a dozen pairs of feet clamored down the steps and then one little girl raced into the kitchen. "Hi, Jake. Whatcha got behind your back?"

She skipped to one side, trying to see, but Jake turned. Kelsey went the other way. Something yipped and Kelsey screeched with glee as Jake brought his arms in front of him, a pudgy, tan-colored puppy in his right hand.

"Oh, Jake, is he for me?"

"It's a she, and I was kinda hoping to talk to your mama about that."

Kelsey twirled toward Josie, the puppy in her thin little arms. "Can I keep her, Mama? Can I?"

The puppy licked Kelsey's neck. Kelsey giggled up a storm, and Josie couldn't help laughing. "I think she's already yours, sweet pea."

"Oh, Mama. Oh, Jake. Thank you, thank you, thank you. What do you think we should name her? Does she already have a name? Isn't she just precious? I hafta think of a name if she doesn't already have one. Oh, Jake, thank you so much."

A thin little arm encircled Jake's neck the second he went down on his haunches. See? Josie thought. Kelsey was thriving. And happy. Sometimes Josie believed she was almost happy, too. She wasn't so sure about Jake.

Something had been different about him these past few weeks. He'd seemed more agitated, and yet when he reached for her at night, there was so much care in his fingertips she was certain he genuinely cared about her. She told herself it was enough. Please, let this be enough.

"When she's bigger, I can teach her tricks. Haley, Jordan and Slade have a dog, but he's real old and doesn't do much. I can read to her. I'm learnin' to read real good, aren't I, Mama? Mama and me are readin' *Little Women*. Mama's mostly readin' it to me on accounta there's lots of hard words. A woman wrote it. Her name's Louisa May somethin' or other. I know. I can name the puppy Louisa.''

Jake scratched the dog underneath the roll of fat on her neck. ''Louie's a good name for her. She's not potty trained yet. Maybe you'd better take her outside and put her down for a minute and see what she does.''

Kelsey's eyes grew so round it was comical. ''Melody's potty training Slade. Oh, Jake. I'll potty train Louie.'' She started for the door, only to run back to Jake one more time. ''Thank you so much.''

''You're welcome.'' He straightened, smiling.

''Come on, Louie. Let's go outside. Finally I have another dog.''

''Another one?'' Jake asked.

Kelsey nodded, her brown eyes, eyes Josie had once said were so like her father's, soft and serene. ''My daddy gave me one when I was little, only me and Mama had to take him to a farm where he could run and play. Right, Mama?''

''That's right, sweet pea.''

The screen door bounced twice. It just so happened that it was the same number of times Jake's heart thudded before returning to a more normal beat.

Tom this. Daddy that.

He swiped his hat off his head, shoved his fingers through his hair. ''I didn't know her father had already given her a dog.''

Josie nodded. ''I'm surprised she remembers. She was so small. We didn't have that dog long enough to teach him any tricks. Tom sure loved that puppy, though. After Tom died, we couldn't afford dog food and vet bills, so we had to give the dog away.''

Tom. Always Tom.

Jake swung around abruptly. "She can keep this one. No matter what happens between you and me."

Without another word he crammed his hat back on his head and left. Josie stood at the table and watched him go, one hand pressed against the smooth wood, the other pressed to her heart.

She'd never asked Jake how long he expected this situation to last, and he'd never said. They hadn't talked about forever. They didn't talk about anything that significant. Now she knew that Jake didn't necessarily expect their marriage to last forever. Of course he didn't. He'd married her to keep his land. She was the one who had fallen in love.

She loved Jake. She'd known it for a while, but she hadn't let the actual words run through her mind as well as her heart. She'd married him to keep Kelsey. She wasn't supposed to fall in love with him. But she hadn't been able to help it. She loved an aloof, distant man who didn't seem able to love her in return.

What am I going to do, Tom?

A bird twittered somewhere. Kelsey giggled, and the puppy barked. The wind whispered through the trees, but Tom didn't answer.

Tom was lost to her; she couldn't look back. Jake held himself apart from her; she couldn't look forward, either. That only left today, and today she saw her husband riding away toward the lane at a full gallop.

A tear trailed down her cheek. Lost and alone, she didn't bother to wipe it away.

"Atta boy." Jake ran his hand down King's broad face. The horse shook his head and snorted. If Jake could have, he would have laughed.

Jake hadn't been doing much laughing lately.

He'd spent an hour racing with the wind and another hour and a half getting back. King had been duly rewarded, his bridle and saddle removed, his coat brushed, his trough filled with fresh water and his bucket with feed and oats. Feeling more amicable, Jake took the flowers he'd picked for Josie and headed for the gate.

Keeping his voice low and soothing, he spoke to Sky's horse on his way past. Bommer did an about-face, presenting Jake with his tail. That horse had never been as forgiving as King. Jake didn't blame him. He knew he'd been a bear lately. Josie knew it, too. He'd seen it on her face and in her eyes. He didn't mean to be so ornery. Hell, he wanted to be nice. Taking her hand-picked wildflowers was only one of the ways he planned to be nice to his wife.

He was halfway to the house when he heard Josie's laughter. Something went soft inside him, luring him like the promise of cool shade on a sweltering day. Josie was out by the road, the mail in one hand, her other hand resting on the open window of Rory O'Grady's truck.

The flowers fell to the brown grass.

Josie must have noticed a movement out of the corner of her eye, because she shaded her eyes with her hand and her laughter stopped. Moments later Rory drove away and Josie walked toward him slowly.

Jake met her halfway. Keeping his voice very low and very controlled, he said, "I've lived these past two months with the fact that I'm standing in the shadow of a dead man, but Rory O'Grady? In the future I would appreciate it if you would be a little more discreet."

"What are you talking about?"

In no mood to stick around or explain, he sped away, anger lengthening his stride.

"Jake, wait."

He didn't so much as glance over his shoulder.

Josie didn't call out to him again. She flinched when she heard the door on the Jeep slam, but she didn't move until he'd pulled out of the shed, gravel spraying beneath his tires.

A splash of color caught her eye. When the Jeep had disappeared down the lane, she walked to the area between the house and the barn where the grass was dry and brown. Bending at the waist, she picked up a bouquet of wilting flowers and slowly brought them to her nose.

She didn't think she could do this anymore. She couldn't live with a man she loved, but who couldn't love her in return.

She didn't know she was crying until Kelsey pressed her little body close to her side. "Do you have an owie, Mama?"

Josie sniffled. "Yes, I guess you could say I do."

"Want me to kiss it and make it better?"

She hugged her little girl, accepting the kiss on her cheek.

"I love you, Mama."

"I love you, too, sweet pea."

"Want me to read you a story?"

Smiling through her tears, Josie said, "I'd like that, Kelsey. Would you like lunch first?"

Kelsey nodded gravely. "Yeah, cuz I'm starving."

That's what Josie had thought. She sent her beautiful daughter a love-filled smile. They strode into the big white house, hand in hand, a chubby tan puppy with bows in her ears and a doll's tutu around her tummy following close behind.

Jake hoisted a bag of feed on one shoulder. Grunting slightly beneath its weight, he carried it to the opposite end of the barn and placed it on the top of the growing stack. The door opened and clattered shut.

"Hey, Kels. What are you doing out here? Where's Louie?"

The child planted her flowered tennis shoes on the dirt floor. She didn't grin or giggle or reply. Her eyes looked red, as if she'd been crying, but it was the accusation in them that made Jake wary. "You okay?" he asked.

"You made Mama cry."

Bommer nickered. Farther away, a calf lowed. Jake didn't know what to say. Since his legs didn't feel fully operational, he stayed where he was and took a couple of deep breaths. "I'm sorry, Kels. I didn't mean to."

"It don't matter if ya meant to. You made her cry, and now we're gonna leave."

The blood drained out of Jake's face. "Did your mother say that?"

The little girl shook her head. "I heard her talkin' on the tel'phone. She asked Mrs. Stryker if she'd subrented our apartment yet. Mama told her not to. I think we're gonna move back. It's all your fault."

With a toss of her head she turned, all raised hackles and feminine grace. Jake's feet were frozen to the floor. He'd made Josie cry and he'd made Kelsey angry. As usual he'd made a mess of pretty much everything.

Any minute now his control was going to snap. He had to get out of there, and he had to do it now.

He made it as far as the barn door before Sky stepped out of the shadows. "You made Josie cry? You're supposed to make a woman laugh, buddy."

Jake swore and promptly changed directions.

He ended up in his dusty black pickup truck, the music blasting, the tires churning up gravel as he sped to no place in particular.

Sky had made it sound so simple. He was supposed to make Josie laugh. She laughed with Kelsey. She laughed with Muriel. She laughed with Sky and Slappy. She was laughing in the picture of her and Tom. She'd laughed with Rory O'Grady. She even laughed with those old hens in the Ladies Aid Society.

And he'd made her cry.

That restless, unwelcome tension came over him, stronger, sharper than ever. He cranked up the music and turned the corner on two wheels.

"You can't shake it, my friend. You can't outrun it. You can't hide from it."

He cranked up the volume and pressed the petal to the floor. The hell he couldn't.

"What did you say sugar?"

Jake glanced up into DoraLee Brown's caring face. He vaguely remembered parking his truck on Main Street and tramping into the Crazy Horse Saloon. Pushing his nearly empty beer bottle away, he said, "Bring me another, DoraLee."

"Are you sure that's wise, McKenna?"

He turned his head quickly and scowled. Rory O'Grady was all he needed.

"I'm not in the mood for company, O'Grady."

Rory wiggled one eyebrow at DoraLee. Damned if he didn't plant himself on the bar stool next to Jake.

"I'll have a beer," he said. "Jake here will have a cup of strong coffee."

"I don't need another conscience, O'Grady. The one I've got is driving me crazy all by itself."

"Good." He winked at DoraLee as she placed a long-necked bottle in front of him and a mug of steaming coffee in front of Jake. DoraLee Brown had been married twice and around the block at least a dozen times, and yet she preened like a schoolgirl at Rory's mild flirtation.

For as long as folks could remember, the O'Gradys had been a good-looking bunch. Besides being the richest ranchers for several hundred miles, they all had black hair and blue eyes and had women eating out of their hands. Rory's two younger brothers looked a lot like him, but Rory was the only O'Grady to sport a mustache and a nose that was the slightest bit crooked, thanks to Jake McKenna.

He raised the beer a few inches off the bar. "To the winner."

A handful of old-timers were playing poker at a table in the back. Otherwise, the bar was quiet. In the ensuing silence, Jake took his time choosing between the last swallow of his beer and the coffee. In the end, he opted not to participate in the toast one way of the other.

"You take life too seriously, McKenna. You kept your land, didn't you?"

"I shouldn't have had to beat my father at his own game."

"Know what I think?" Rory asked.

"Pray tell."

Rory had never been one to let a little sarcasm faze him. "I think your old man cared about you." At Jake's derisive snort, Rory said, "I mean it. Oh, Isaac wasn't worth a damn at saying it or showing it, but I think he put that stipulation in his will because he didn't want his hard-headed, ornery, grouchy, scowling..."

"If you've got a point, make it, O'Grady."

"As I was saying. He didn't want his snarling, bear of a son to end up old and lonely like he did. Isaac knew how you felt about us, so he sweetened the pot, so to speak."

Jake turned his head slowly to look at the other man.

"You don't think for a minute that he really believed

you would let your precious land go to us, do you?'' Rory touched the bridge of his nose. ''I shouldn't have said what I said about your mother. When we were kids. I was jealous. Guess I still am.''

Jake eyed the last swallow of beer in the bottle. That one had been his first and only drink, so he couldn't have been drunk. Therefore he couldn't have been hearing things.

''You don't believe me?'' Rory asked. ''Of course I'm jealous. Okay, maybe I'm not jealous. I am an O'Grady after all. But I am envious. You're the one who got the girl.''

''We both know why Josie married me.''

Rory leaned closer just in case one of the old men in the back had turned up his hearing aid and was trying to eavesdrop. ''You think she married you for money? Security? If that's all there was to it, she would have married me.'' He held up both hands. ''Before you break my nose again, I might as well tell you that I offered Josie twice whatever you were giving her. I think she loves you. I guess there's no accounting for taste.''

That unwelcome tension settled over Jake's head like a big, black rain cloud. He didn't try to outrun it. He didn't try to outride it. This time he didn't hide. What was the use?

Rory dropped a couple of bills on the counter and left. Jake was left sitting all by himself at the bar beneath a dark cloud that had been following him around most of his life.

Was it possible that his father had loved him? Was it possible that Josie loved him?

When she'd agreed to marry him, he'd felt a crack in the outer layer of his heart. He'd done everything in his power to seal it back up.

A flash of lightning bolted out of that storm cloud, forking straight through his chest. He placed his hands flat on the bar, shoving himself up. He couldn't move. For a moment the thought he was having a heart attack. But his heart was beating. He could feel it. It was as if there was a second crack in his heart in the same place the first had been, this one wider and deeper than the first.

He'd cemented his heart up good and tight over the years. It had taken a pale-faced woman with red hair and a flare of temper to open it along with his eyes.

Kelsey had said they were leaving.

A sudden burning need overtook him. He had to talk to Josie. Before it was too late.

Chapter Eleven

It was already too late. Jake felt it all the way to his bones. His bones had to be wrong. It couldn't be too late.

He'd just come from his lawyer's office in Pierre. Jamison Maxwell had been the McKenna's attorney for as long as Jake could remember. The man was as thin as a rail and as mean as Isaac. He was shrewd and hadn't appreciated being silenced by Jake's command, "Just do it, Jamison. Or you're fired."

It had taken a while to get the wording right, and the legal description had been tricky. When he'd finally pulled away from the curb, the document Jake had gone after was sitting beside him on the seat.

He prayed he wasn't too late.

He sped into the driveway and pulled to a stop, leaving the truck at a cockeyed angle. He scanned the porch, the corral, the yard. Josie's car was still here. He took that as a good sign.

The first thing he noticed when he set foot in the house

were the bags, packed and ready, near the door. Not a good sign. But if their bags and car were still here, Josie and Kelsey must be, too.

He didn't find them anywhere in the house, but he saw signs of their imminent departure everywhere. There were no flowers in jelly jars, no stones in chipped teacups, no crayon artwork on the refrigerator. There was something warming in the oven, though. It humbled him to know that she'd thought about him even as she prepared to leave.

He found them underneath a shade tree behind the house. Josie was sitting on an old quilt, her back against the tree, Kelsey curled up close to her, sound asleep. Josie must have chosen the spot for its ambiance, because the sun wasn't out, and there was no need for a shady spot. The sky was dull and gray with the promise of rain, or gloom, depending on one's perspective.

For a long time he simply stared, putting her to memory. He strode closer, the breeze stirring the document in his left hand. He removed his hat with his other hand and tried to think of something poignant and thought provoking to say.

"I think it's finally going to rain."

He scowled. He was hopeless. No wonder Josie didn't respond.

"Do you think Kels will care that Louie's chewing through her doll's leg?"

Josie smiled, albeit sadly, and ran her hand along the dog's soft fur. "Kelsey gave her that doll."

Kels was a generous little kid. She took after her mother. "Noticed your bags are packed."

She nodded, and he thought she looked tired. There was silence between them again. Jake didn't know how to fill it. He wasn't used to having to do all the talking. He wasn't very good at talking. Cole had been the talker in the family.

He wanted to put his hands in his pockets, but his hands were full, so he settled for lowering them to his sides. "I was afraid you'd be gone when I got here."

"I told Kelsey we didn't have to go until we finished reading *Little Women*."

The book lay open to the last page.

"Don't go."

She stared up at him, her green eyes filled with tears.

"I have to, Jake." Josie took a shuddering breath, willing herself to remain strong just a little while longer. Trying on a smile that felt out of place, she said, "You're probably wishing Crystal had said yes, huh?"

She saw the surprise on Jake's face. As one second followed another, she saw understanding dawn, as well.

"I'm sorry about a lot of things, Josephine, but I'm not sorry you're the one who said yes."

Josie squeezed her eyes shut. She thought she could live through just about anything, but hearing him say "Josephine" made her ache from the backs of her eyes all the way to the bottom of her heart.

His boots crunched on the dry grass as he walked closer; the papers clutched so tight in his hand crinkled in the breeze. "I probably should have told you this in the first place. There are a lot of things I probably should have told you. I thought I was better at showing you. Guess I was wrong."

She opened her eyes and found that he'd hunkered down near her, the tips of his boots even with the edge of the quilt. "I never asked Crystal Galloway to marry me. You're the only woman I've ever proposed to. The only one."

It wasn't easy to keep her hands in her lap, when she so wanted to touch his lean face. "Oh, Jake."

He stood up fast and started to pace. "I know I have no right to ask you to stay. I'm asking, anyway. I'll beg, barter, steal if I have to. Stay."

"Jake. Don't. This isn't working. You're miserable. You get more agitated every day. I think you need more than a marriage of convenience, on your need to keep your land and my need to keep Kelsey."

An unwelcome tension took hold of him again. This time he met it head-on and looked it in the eye. He'd been a fool, and unless he did something, and did something soon, she was going to leave, just like everyone else he'd loved had done.

"I told you I never missed Nadine." Jake stopped short. Where in the hell had that come from? He turned around just as Josie was rising to her feet, graceful and beautiful in one of the dresses he'd seen a dozen times before. She was watching him with the same kind of soft expression he'd seen when she looked at Kelsey. He wasn't some little kid, dammit, in need of a mother's touch.

Aw, hell. "I missed her. My mother. For a long time after she left."

"You were a child, Jake. You deserved better than what she gave you. You deserved her love. I love you, you know."

Jake staggered backward, righted himself and stared. Rory had said she probably loved him. Hearing Josie say it rendered him speechless all over again. In lieu of a better plan, he shoved the paper into her hands.

"What's this?"

"It's a quit claim deed, turning the hundred acres that spans Sugar Creek over to you. Before you tear it in half or throw it back in my face, you might as well know that you own half of the ranch, anyway.''

She took her turn at becoming speechless. Jake rather enjoyed it. "I never had a prenuptial agreement drawn up, Josie. Half of the Lone M became yours the day you married me.''

"I never wanted your money, Jake. Or your land.''

"Tough. You have both.''

"I won't accept them.''

There were twin pink splotches on her cheeks. It wasn't from embarrassment. He'd ticked her off. Good. At least they were getting somewhere.

He resumed pacing. "You wouldn't take money from me unless you'd earned it. Why the hell not? I asked myself. That was what husbands did. Supported their families.''

"I need a husband who's willing to do more than support me.''

He stopped pacing suddenly. "What do you mean?''

"I want a man who talks to me." She lifted one eyebrow sardonically. "You seem to have mastered talking.''

He felt his eyes narrow. She was right. The words he'd had so much trouble saying for years had rolled out his mouth with very little effort. "What else do you want in a man, Josie?''

She took care walking closer, sidestepping Kelsey and the puppy. "I want a man who is open with me, about his dreams, his feelings. I know that isn't easy for a lot of men, and it's harder for you than for most.''

Jake thought about the tears he'd seen on her face when he'd crept out of their bed on their wedding night. Those tears had been for Tom. He thought about how he'd felt. She wanted to know his secrets, his feelings. He couldn't come close to putting how he felt about Tom into words and still retain his pride and his manhood. He'd felt as if he'd come in second all his life. At first to Cole and then to Tom.

He'd once told Josie that Thomas Callahan had been a lucky man. He still believed that. But Tom must have been a good man, too, because Josie had loved him. He'd also been smart. Smart enough to know what he wanted, and strong enough to turn his back on his controlling parents and go after what he wanted. He'd wanted Josie's love, and he'd had it. A part of her would probably always love him. Strangely, that didn't seem to mean she loved Jake any less.

Maybe life wasn't a race, with winners and losers and second places.

Jake thought about the stipulation his father had put in his will. Had Isaac cared about him after all? And he thought about the money Josie had refused, the deed she was refusing even now, and the bags that were packed and waiting by the door. She'd told him she loved him. He leaned toward believing her. Why else would she have refused everything of monetary value? She'd said it a half-dozen times. She didn't want his money. What she'd failed to spell out for him was that she wanted his love.

He finally figured something out. It wasn't who you loved first or last. The important thing was to love with everything you had, and to be loved in return.

"I love you, Josephine," he said, reaching for her hand.

He saw her lips quiver and wanted to cover them with his own. But he wouldn't. Not yet, because once he did, words might escape him. And he still had a few things to say. Lifting her hand, he placed it on his chest. "You laugh with Kelsey. You laugh with Muriel and Melody and Sky and Slappy. But you never laugh with me."

Josie felt tears brim in her eyes. She let them spill over. Jake loved her. And he was sharing a part of himself he'd never shared with another living soul.

She felt honored, and humbled, and terrified she might do or say the wrong thing now that they were so close to working things out. "I want to laugh with you, Jake. Say something funny."

The surprise on his face was almost comical. He grasped her shoulders, spun her around, then spun around himself. "I'll be right back."

Jake ran all the way to the bunkhouse. "Sky! Buchanan! Where are you?"

Sky came out of the bedroom, his chest and feet bare, sleep in his eyes.

"She wants me to make her laugh."

"Good for her."

"I need your help."

Sky scratched his chest and then a spot that was difficult to reach on the back of his shoulder. "Buddy, I thought you'd never ask."

Clouds were churning overhead when Jake returned to the backyard. Feeling as nervous as a naughty boy on Christmas morning, he folded his arms, unfolded them, planted his hands on his hips, then folded his arms again. He should have asked Sky about the delivery. No time for that now.

"Three men are playing golf. Moses, his best friend, and a very old man. Moses tees up first. Or was it his best friend?"

Josie felt herself smiling. Not because of the joke. She had no idea where that was going. Not even because of the topic, although she doubted Jake had ever played golf in his life. She smiled at the earnest expression on his face.

She'd bet her half of the ranch that he hadn't told a joke in a very long time.

She felt the first sprinkle about the same time Jake muttered, "Oh, hell, I forgot the punch line. It wasn't that funny anyway. Hold on. Here's another. Three men were stranded on a desert island. A rodeo champion, a clown, and a beauty contest judge." He stopped abruptly, and scowled. "The men all laughed when Billy told it out on the range, but it's hardly a joke fit for a lady."

"Jake?"

"Don't worry, I'll come up with something."

"Jake?"

He stopped his pacing, and met her gaze.

"Laughter isn't all I want."

He looked down into her face. "It isn't?"

She shook her head.

Emotions stirred inside Jake. There was so much heat in Josie's eyes, warmth stirred everyplace else. He was tempted to kiss her, here and now. My, was he tempted. Instead, he leaned close, and whispered, "Have I told you that I love you, Josephine? I love Kelsey, too, and your flowers, and coming home to the two of you at the end of the day. And have I ever mentioned that your laughter reminds me of birdsong?"

Josie smiled through her tears. And here she'd thought he was a man of few words.

He lowered his face as she raised hers. Their lips met in a kiss as soft as the rain soaking into their clothes. Thunder rumbled, and Jake and Josie drew apart. They laughed as they raced to the quilt. Jake scooped Kelsey into his arms; Josie right behind him with a wriggling tan puppy. They reached the porch just as thunder rumbled again. It wasn't raining hard yet, but suddenly it appeared to be a promising day.

"Jake!" Kelsey blinked the sleep from her eyes. "You're here."

"I'm here, Kels."

"Are we gonna stay, Mama?"

"We're going to stay, sweet pea."

"Goody. And can I call Jake, Daddy?"

Josie and Jake shared a long look. Together, they both nodded.

The fist that had wrapped around Jake's heart so many years ago loosened. Ba-boom. And then, what felt like five minutes later, ba-boom, ba-boom, ba-boom.

A sudden gust of wind came out of nowhere. It whipped through their clothes, as if getting their attention, only to die away to little more than a whisper. It was a low croon, a deep sigh. It reminded Jake of the new voice he'd been hearing in his conscience.

"That sounded like my other daddy's voice," Kelsey declared. "Did you hear it, Mama?"

Josie listened intently. "All I hear is the wind, Kelsey." But she smiled, because the breeze trailing across her face felt a little like a gentle kiss goodbye.

Jake looked at Josie. At Kelsey.

"Did you hear it?" Kelsey asked from her perch in Jake's arms.

Hear it, he thought to himself. He'd been hearing it for months. It had been driving him absolutely crazy. He'd thought it was his conscience. "It couldn't have been your Tom, could it?" he asked.

Josie stared up at her husband's strong, hard face. He was trying to smile, the lift of his lips so tentative it brought tears to her eyes, and strong emotion to her heart. All these months he'd been hurting her with his silence because *he'd* been hurting. He'd felt second-best all his life. He'd felt it with her, as well.

Everything inside Josie started to swirl together. All her thoughts turned to oblivion, all her needs became one. And there, in the center of everything, was Jake.

"He's not my Tom anymore. I haven't heard his voice in months. Not since before our wedding. Not since I fell in love with you. You're the man in my heart, Jake. You're the man in my dreams. Tom was my past, but you are my today."

"You wouldn't go back?" he asked.

She shook her head, her gaze sweeping from her daughter to her husband. "There's a reason we can't, Jake. Besides, I'd rather go forward, into tomorrow, with you."

Thunder rumbled again just as Jake touched his lips to Josie's, a curious little girl and a wiggly puppy between them. When Kelsey squirmed, Jake put her down, her bare feet pattering on the floor as she helped Louie onto the porch swing.

With his heart beating so loud he was sure Josie could hear, Jake wrapped an arm around her shoulder and drew her to his side. "I remember the punch line, now. Care to hear the rest of that joke?"

Josie listened; her eyes grew large as he spun words into mental pictures designed to make people laugh. He bobbled the punch line a little, but it didn't matter. Her heart swelled with love, and she started to laugh. Kelsey giggled just for the fun of it, and Louie barked.

Jake looked out into the night, and then at the woman and child he wanted to share his land and his life with. He didn't know what he'd done to deserve either of them, but he vowed to spend the rest of his life being the best husband and father he could be. They loved him. It was an amazing feeling, being loved. It was the best feeling in the world.

The puppy was playing tug-of-war with Kelsey's sleeve. The little girl giggled happily. It was so comical, Josie joined in. Jake had wrapped his arm around her waist a few minutes ago. Now, as if it was the most natural thing in the world, she threaded her arm around his waist, and gently laid her head on his shoulder.

Jake closed his eyes at the sheer rightness of the moment. His chest felt so full, he laughed, too.

The clouds opened up, and all of heaven joined in.

* * * * *

Look for Sandra Steffen's next story,
A CHRISTMAS TO TREASURE,
part of Silhouette Books'
DELIVERED BY CHRISTMAS *collection,*
available in December.

Silhouette ROMANCE™

VIRGIN BRIDES

**Your favorite authors
tell more heartwarming
stories of lovely brides
who discover love...
for the first time....**

July 1999 GLASS SLIPPER BRIDE
Arlene James (SR #1379)
Bodyguard Jack Keller had to protect innocent
Jillian Waltham—day and night. But when his assignment
became a matter of temporary marriage, would Jack's hardened
heart need protection...from Jillian, his glass slipper bride?

September 1999 MARRIED TO THE SHEIK
Carol Grace (SR #1391)
Assistant Emily Claybourne secretly loved her boss, and now Sheik
Ben Ali had finally asked her to marry him! But Ben was only
interested in a temporary union...until Emily started showing him
the joys of marriage—and love....

November 1999 THE PRINCESS AND THE COWBOY
Martha Shields (SR #1403)
When runaway Princess Josephene Francoeur needed a
short-term husband, cowboy Buck Buchanan was the perfect
choice. But to wed him, Josephene had to tell a *few* white lies,
which worked...until "Josie Freeheart" realized she wanted
to love her rugged cowboy groom forever!

Available at your favorite retail outlet.

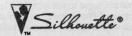

If you enjoyed what you just read,
then we've got an offer you can't resist!

Take 2 bestselling
love stories FREE!
Plus get a FREE surprise gift!

THE FORTUNES OF TEXAS

*Membership in this family has
its privileges...and its price.
But what a fortune can't buy,
a true-bred Texas love is sure to bring!*

Coming in November 1999...

Expecting...
In Texas
by

MARIE FERRARELLA

Wrangler Cruz Perez's night of passion with Savannah Clark
had left the beauty pregnant with his child. Cruz's cowboy
code of honor demanded he do right by the expectant
mother, but could he convince Savannah—and himself—
that his offer of marriage was inspired by true love?

THE FORTUNES OF TEXAS continues with
A Willing Wife by Jackie Merritt,
available in December 1999 from
Silhouette Books.

Available at your favorite retail outlet.

Of all the unforgettable families created by
#1 *New York Times* bestselling author

NORA ROBERTS

the Donovans are the most extraordinary. For, along with
their irresistible appeal, they've inherited some rather
remarkable gifts from their Celtic ancestors.

Coming in November 1999

THE DONOVAN LEGACY

3 full-length novels in one special volume:

CAPTIVATED: Hardheaded skeptic Nash Kirkland has *always*
kept his feelings in check, until he falls under the bewitching
spell of mysterious Morgana Donovan.

ENTRANCED: Desperate to find a missing child, detective
Mary Ellen Sutherland dubiously enlists beguiling
Sebastian Donovan's aid and discovers his uncommon abilities
include a talent for seduction.

CHARMED: Enigmatic healer Anastasia Donovan would do
anything to save the life of handsome Boone Sawyer's
daughter, even if it means revealing her secret to the man
who'd stolen her heart.

Also in November 1999 from Silhouette Intimate Moments

ENCHANTED

Lovely, guileless Rowan Murray is drawn to darkly enigmatic
Liam Donovan with a power she's never imagined possible. But
before Liam can give Rowan his love, he must first reveal to
her his incredible secret.

▼ *Silhouette*®
™

Available at your favorite retail outlet.

PSNRDLR